"Tracy, we've always been b...

Leigh's voi... ...er
since we we...
other every...

Not quite everything, Tracy thought
grimly. *I haven't told you I'm seeing Ryle
Tanner again.*

Leigh made a wide, sweeping gesture with
her arms. "So who else would I confide in?
Especially now that you're back in Council
Grove to stay."

"Okay, Leigh, who is he? Who's this
wonderful new man you're so smitten with?
You...you said I used to know him."
Tracy tried hard to sound cheerful but her
throat was tight with fear. *Please not Ryle.
Don't let it be Ryle.*

"You sure did know him," Leigh burst out.
"You even dated him for a while. I'm
surprised you haven't guessed yet. It's Ryle
Tanner!"

Tracy swallowed painfully. *Tell her,* she
warned herself. *You have to tell her before
it's too late.*

Virginia Hart comes from a family of writers. Her sister writes mysteries, and her husband—who's even more romantic than Virginia's "heroes"—is an award-winning country music songwriter. Virginia, not to be outdone, has written mysteries, historical romances, Westerns and now Harlequin Romances. Confusion is the order of the day at the Harts' Burbank, California, home, with Virginia at her typewriter, cola in hand—she says she's addicted—and her husband composing and singing at the top of his lungs. Their two sons, no doubt, add to the creative chaos.

Books by Virginia Hart

Night of the Spring Moon

Virginia Hart

Harlequin Books

TORONTO • NEW YORK • LONDON
AMSTERDAM • PARIS • SYDNEY • HAMBURG
STOCKHOLM • ATHENS • TOKYO • MILAN

ISBN 0-373-02882-2

Harlequin Romance first edition January 1988

CHAPTER ONE

THE SIGHT OF THE OLD COURTHOUSE wrenched Tracy into the reality of being home again. Home. Her first impulse was to make a U-turn and go back the way she had come. But she didn't give in to it.

The white-painted building with its railed porches and fluted columns was one of the oldest in Missouri. Deep pits showed where Confederate bullets had bitten into the walls, bearing witness to the tragic battle waged there more than a century before.

Tracy had waged a battle of her own in Council Grove. Maybe it didn't show, but she, too, still carried the scars.

Garfield Park had swallowed up the Just-Rite Tea Company that used to squat next to it and was now twice the size it had been when she was a child. The park grass was carefully clipped and lush from the recent spring rains. She and Leigh Monahan, her best friend, had spent countless hours sitting beside the old cannon, sharing girlhood secrets and trying to find four-leaf clovers.

Did children still do that?

Tracy had always found the most. But never the good luck that was said to go with them.

Enough! Now was not the time for bitterness or regrets. Returning home was her own decision, and it was one she'd made very carefully. She knew she'd have to confront her past if she was going to live here again. She had no illusions about that. Gossip lingered for years in small towns like this; it never really disappeared, just became part of the local mythology. But Council Grove was *home*, in a way no other place had ever been.

Her nine-year-old brother, who'd been dozing on the seat beside her, sat up and blinked. "Where are we?" he asked in a drowsy voice. His arms were still tightly wrapped around Willie, their shaggy part poodle, part terrier.

"We're here."

He glanced sullenly around, his mouth pulled down at the corners. "You're kidding."

"Do I look as if I'm kidding? No, Michael, m'lad. This is Council Grove. See that gigantic granddaddy of a tree over there? Years ago, Indians would hold their council meetings under it. Hence, the name of the town."

Michael wasn't impressed. "Where are the buildings?"

"Around us. And feast your eyes on that delicious swimming pool. It wasn't here when I left. All we had was the muddy pond at Fletcher's Corner."

"Big deal. What about baseball?"

"They've heard of baseball here, Michael. Trust me."

"I'm starving."

"Me too."

"Let's eat. There's a place." He pointed.

A restaurant in the shape of an enormous hot dog now stood where the Olive Five and Dime had once been. Tracy clenched her teeth. The place was filled to overflowing. She expected to encounter her old neighbors—and one-time friends—sooner or later. But she'd rather it were later.

"My stomach's growling," Michael wailed.

His pleading won out. He was grouchy already and she couldn't blame him. They'd been on the road since early morning, so he was not only hungry but tired and cramped. And she knew he was more than a little nervous. This was the fourth time in his young life that his roots had been transplanted. For the fourth time, he'd had to leave everything behind—his school, his neighborhood, his friends—and start all over again. Not that he ever had many friends; Michael was a loner. But changes were traumatic, something Tracy had learned ten years before. She'd just have to humor him, she decided. She'd make this transition as easy for him as she could.

For the sake of her self-esteem, she avoided her reflection in the rearview mirror. The air-conditioning had given up fifty miles out of Kansas City. Her tan shirt was stuck to her back and her khaki pants were creased and rumpled. Her honey-brown hair was limp and straight and she'd chewed off her lipstick.

"Tray—cee!" Michael prodded.

"Okay, okay. Keep your T-shirt on." She gave a hand signal, remembering that her signal lights didn't work, then turned and angled the Plymouth between, if not exactly parallel to, the slanting white lines.

Tracy rolled up the windows while Michael reassured the whimpering dog. As they clambered out of the car, waving goodbye to Willie, a vintage truck wheezed by and slowed momentarily before continuing its course. Was the driver someone she used to know? Someone who recognized her and wondered what Tracy Whelan was doing back in Council Grove?

She pushed the question from her mind as they entered the restaurant. Its cooling system was on full force, but the chill was welcome. The smell of roasting hot dogs tickled her appetite, and the midafternoon mob appeared to be made up of strangers. So far, so good.

Besides, she reminded herself, she'd changed in ten years. A late bloomer, she hadn't really filled out until she was almost twenty. Mascara on her long, thick, but somewhat pale eyelashes had widened her gray-green eyes. And her hair was entirely different. In those days, she had simply parted it in the middle and allowed it to hang straight and loose to her shoulders. Now her hair was inches shorter, curled at the ends and parted on one side. Curled, that is, on days when she wasn't hot, exhausted and nervous.

She was standing at the counter, spreading mustard on her hot dog and trying to decide if she wanted onions, when the door flew open and slapped shut again with a bang. "Who belongs to the yellow Plymouth?" someone bellowed.

Tracy didn't look up until Michael tugged at her sleeve. "Uh-oh. That's us."

Peering through the crowd of customers behind her, she caught only a glimpse of the man who'd asked the question. At least he wasn't wearing a sheriff's uniform, which probably meant they weren't in danger of imminent arrest. But he was definitely hostile. He was moving purposefully toward the counter now, and all her hopes of keeping a low profile went up in smoke. Dozens of pairs of eyes were fixed on her. She noticed how willingly the other customers stepped aside to let the man through, muttering to each other and shaking their heads. "Who the hell owns that car?" he demanded a second time.

Her face flamed with embarrassment. "It's mine," she said. Her voice came out sounding like a poor imitation of Snow White. She cleared her throat and tried again. "It's ours."

"Then I assume the shaggy pup is yours, too."

"Yes." Oh, no. It was Ryle Tanner. Ryle. She recognized him instantly, though the years had darkened his hair a shade or two and added a lot of weight and muscle to his frame. He was still rangy, but his build was impressive and powerful looking. Even if he'd gained two hundred pounds and gone bald, she'd have known him. She remembered his Gunfight-at-the-OK-Corral walk and the way he squinted one eye when he was angry. She remembered, too, that defiant gunslinger's stance, feet planted wide apart, hands on hips.

"If you plan to get rid of him," Ryle went on, "take him to the animal shelter on Sixth and have it done humanely."

"Now wait a darn minute, Tanner," she shot back, her defense mechanism taking over.

"No. You wait, lady." He jabbed a finger at her. "I'm always tempted to smash a car window when I see a helpless animal shut up in a hot car. Do you have any conception of how high the temperature soars when you're parked in the sun? Do you know..." He squinted still more and slapped a hand to his forehead. "Tracy?"

"Yes. Tracy. And yes, I was wrong to leave Willie shut in the car like that. It was stupid of me. I closed the windows so he couldn't get out—I wasn't thinking. But we were only planning to be gone for about ten minutes."

"A car can turn into Hades in *one* minute. You could have come back to a dead dog. If the door hadn't been unlocked and I hadn't been able to lower a window a few inches to give him air—"

"I'm sorry," she interrupted, not in the mood for a lecture, especially a public one—no matter how deserved. She looked at her brother, who was wiping mustard from his chin with a paper napkin. "You've finished your hot dog already? I don't believe it."

Michael nodded. "You want yours?"

She shook her head. "Help yourself. But don't gulp the whole thing down in two bites this time." Ryle's attack had robbed her of her appetite. "Why not go out and check on Willie, too? I won't be long."

Ryle took her elbow and steered her out of the way of two boys who were attempting to reach over her shoulder to get to the relish. "You're here visiting Leigh Monahan?"

It was hardly a brilliant deduction, since he knew that Leigh was one of the only people in town who'd stood by Tracy through the trouble. "Not exactly. I'm here to stay." There. She'd said it.

He stared at his hands, frowning, as he considered her answer. "Oh?"

That was all he could find to say? *Oh?* Wasn't he even a *little* pleased to see her again?

"So, you're still the mighty crusader for the rights of the four-footed," she said, ignoring the implications of his less-than-effusive welcome. "Did you become a vet as you planned?"

"Did you think I wouldn't?"

"No. I remember how determined you were."

He glanced up quickly. "So were you."

She'd forgotten about his eyes. How could she have? They were the darkest shade of brown—almost black— she'd ever seen, testament to the fact that he was one-quarter Blackfoot. But what had always fascinated her was the incredible depth of those eyes. They seemed not just to touch but to transfix hers. It was a sensation that made her feel almost giddy.

Ryle had always been completely huggable, even in the old days, when he was thin and really rather gawky. Even then he'd been what the girls called "cute." Now he was much, much more. Thank heavens he couldn't guess that the sight of him had stirred the primitive instincts of her woman's body. Or could he? She released her breath a bit at a time, steadily, not wanting him to realize that she'd been unconsciously holding it.

She couldn't shrug off what she was feeling as "auld lang syne." No matter how she tried, she wasn't able to stop her physical appraisal of him. Of the breadth of his shoulders. Of the way his muscular thighs shaped the slim legs of his jeans. Of... The turn her thoughts were taking made her face feel flushed and hot. She dragged her attention back to the comparative safety of his face. Fortunately he was too busy conducting an inventory of his own to have noticed hers.

"Did you ever explore those ruins of ancient civilizations?" he asked, his voice a little friendlier now.

She thought back. He was right. At one time, her burning ambition had been to become an archaeologist. "The only ruins I've explored were those I saw when I was apartment-hunting for something I could afford. No. That childhood dream was packed away with my Barbie dolls. I'm a hairdresser."

He didn't comment, but he wasn't missing her disheveled hairdo, either.

Instinctively her hand flew up, smoothing back damp strands of hair. "It's hot in the car."

"That's what your dog told me, too."

She groaned. He was still Ryle. Even when he'd won an argument hands down he wouldn't let go of it. "I've already apologized and sent Michael to the car. What more do you want me to do?"

"Apologize to Willie and tell him it won't happen again."

Programmed by years of feeling the need to defend herself, she half wanted to snap a biting retort. But he was smiling, a heart-stopping, slow smile. Suddenly she couldn't speak, and for no apparent reason, tears sprang into her eyes.

"Are you crying?"

No diplomat, Ryle. She blinked, embarrassed. "It doesn't mean anything. I was always a weeper. I bawl over happy movies as well as sad ones. I can even soak a Kleenex over a good preview."

"I don't remember that about you." His tongue slid across the edge of his squarish lower teeth as he weighed her explanation.

What do you remember, Ryle? she asked silently. Scott Barclay? The fires?

She and Ryle had dated for most of her junior year. She'd cared so much for him. She liked his serious face and his straight short nose. She liked the way one of his eyebrows would peak when he was puzzled about something or deep in thought. She liked his droll sense of humor and his sharply defined mouth. She liked the way his hand felt when it held hers and the way his hair took on pale streaks when he spent any time in the sun. Best of all, she liked their long comfortable hours together, talking, laughing, arguing...loving.

But Ryle had been almost three years older and light years more dedicated to his ambition. He'd been so engrossed in studying—chemistry, physics—so many difficult subjects, he hadn't given her much time. It was always, "You know we can't go tonight, honey. I have to hit the books." Or, "Can you see that movie with Leigh? I have an exam tomorrow."

When he'd canceled their date for the biggest school dance of the year to attend some 4-H happening in Moberly, she'd been furious. So she'd gone to the dance with Scott Barclay to make Ryle jealous. When Ryle took it in his stride and didn't react, when he seemed not to care one way or the other, she switched to Scott completely.

Scott came from one of *the* families in town. He was good-looking and popular. Yet, unlike Ryle, he seemed to need her. There was a strange complicity between Scott and Tracy; he showed his vulnerable side only to her and allowed her to share his secrets. But only some of them. She'd discovered that last secret for herself—when it was too late.

She was jarred back to the present by Michael, who was gesturing and making faces at her through the restaurant window. With the wriggling dog in his arms, he opened the door. "Tracy, can I take Willie for a run in the park?"

"Don't bring that mutt in here. People are eating," the counterman yelled, and again heads turned. "Get him outside."

"Put a leash on him first, son, if you're going to walk him," Ryle said.

Michael didn't answer, but he shot Tracy a what's-it-got-to-do-with-him look.

"The leash," she seconded. "He might dash into the street and get hit by a car."

"In this town?" The boy rolled his eyes skyward. "More like a horse and buggy."

Ryle shifted his weight from one foot to the other. He was getting edgy, Tracy decided, and didn't know how to back off gracefully. He didn't care to be seen with her. It was up to her to bring this embarrassing encounter to a close.

"Well, Tanner." She offered him her hand and a wide smile. "I want you to know I'm proud of you." He would thank her, she would tell him she'd probably see him around, and that would be that.

"Proud?" He accepted the hand, pressed it, and brushed his thumb lightly across her knuckles before releasing it.

Had she read him wrong? Warmth engulfed her and she averted her face, not wanting him to see the confusion and the longing in her eyes.

Why hadn't she worn something pretty and provocative for her return? Something that would have drawn a silent, appreciative whistle from the good doctor? Something more snug, to define the gentle curves she deprived herself of hot-fudge sundaes to maintain? Something with a little more color, to light up her face—and his eyes.

She might at least have combed her hair.

"I've heard it's a real feat to be accepted by a veterinary college. Not to mention the horrendous expense," she said. "Naturally I'm proud."

And she was. She knew that Ryle's parents hadn't been able to afford the tuition. His father had retired early because of a back injury and his mother had worked as a practical nurse. That meant he'd put himself through school. He'd made it on his own.

"The scholarship helped." His voice was deep and hesitant, as if there was a need to make each word count. "My parents couldn't pay for my education, but the things they taught me money can't buy." He paused. "They've moved, by the way. They live in Florida now, and I have the house. I don't see them much anymore, but we talk on the phone quite often." He glanced at Tracy, then looked away as he mumbled, "They'll be glad to hear you're back in town. They always liked you."

She was touched by what he'd said about his parents. At the same time she felt like grabbing him by the collar and shouting, "Yeah, but what about *you*? Did you still like me after everything that happened?" She wondered if he'd been one of those who'd judged her unfairly. Had he, too, decided she was guilty without waiting to hear her side of the story?

Her feelings must have been clearly visible on her face, because he was watching her very carefully now. In her eagerness to distract him, she blurted out the first question she could think of, almost stumbling over the words. "So, what comes next in your life story? After college I mean."

"I was lucky enough to make a deal with Doc Cole," he drawled, moving his sensuous, full lower lip in a way that made her want to kiss it.

Remembering how much she detested people who watched her mouth as she spoke, she forced her eyes away. "Doc Cole is still around?"

"Livelier than ever. I'm buying his practice a little at a time. Working with him every minute I wasn't studying taught me things I couldn't possibly have learned in a classroom. Being seen with him helped me to build up a trust among the farmers he's known a lifetime. He's retiring inch by inch. Eventually I'll take over completely."

"A perfect ending to your story. Or should I say beginning?" Tracy said and instantly regretted the words. She hadn't meant to sound so frivolous. She suddenly wished she were wearing sunglasses, preferably the mirrored kind that would have concealed her eyes—and her feelings.

"Never mind me for a moment. It's your turn to tell a story now. Tell me about Tracy Whelan." He took her arm and pushed open the door, leading her outside.

As they crossed the street to the park, she told him about the salon in Kansas City where she'd worked after she got her license, and about her parents' disappointment when she decided against business college and eventual partnership in their insurance agency.

"They saw beauty operators as they're portrayed in old movies. You know. Gum-snapping, floozy types with overbleached hair and a jiggly walk? I couldn't make them understand that hairdressing is really something I want to do. It's fulfilling for me. I consider it an art."

"You could look at it that way," he agreed. "Anyhow, it's safer than robbing Egyptian tombs."

"I had some savings bonds my grandfather left me," she went on. "That was a start. Then I squirreled away every penny I earned toward the day I could realize my dream. My own shop. I could have settled in Kansas City, but everything is so much more expensive there. It would have taken years longer. The competition is keener, too. There seems to be a salon on every other block. Besides, I was very happy in Council Grove once and I knew I could be again."

She was silent for a moment, not sure how much to tell him. It wasn't really any of his business, she decided, feeling an obscure need to protect herself—from what? From Ryle, or from her own reaction to this man she hadn't seen in ten years? "Anyway," she resumed, "Leigh and I discussed it in letter after letter. I finally made a decision, she located a site for me and here I am."

Ryle snapped his fingers. "The vacant store on Front Street. I heard someone took it over."

"I understand it isn't much. But it's a beginning."

"We'll be neighbors. I'm right around the corner."

"Hi, neighbor," Tracy said, giving him a cheery little wave.

When she smiled at him, he smiled back—an unreserved smile this time. "Are your folks coming here, too?"

"No." Tracy drew a long breath to steady herself. "My father died four years ago."

"I'm sorry. I didn't know."

"He'd had a heart condition for some time. We'd been expecting it. But I guess you're never truly prepared to lose someone you love, are you?"

"No, you aren't."

"The medical bills were staggering. Mother had to sell the house and we moved to a tiny apartment closer to the city. Michael was only five then—too young to understand why his father suddenly just disappeared from his life."

"And now?"

"Mother remarried a few months ago. She and her new husband are taking a belated honeymoon cruise."

"And you're in charge of Michael while they're gone?"

"Well . . . yes. Frank, the man mother married, is a good person, but he's rather reserved and he isn't used to children. He and Michael clashed horribly from the start. It didn't help that they moved again, to a new neighborhood, miles away from the old one. Michael began throwing temper tantrums and at school he was in one scrape after another."

"Fighting back at life in his own way."

Tracy nodded. "Frank would want to discipline him, Mother would step in and next thing you knew, they'd be fighting about it."

"Not a great start for a marriage," Ryle said.

"No. It couldn't have lasted between them the way things were going. I managed to convince my mother that Michael would be better off making his home with me, for the next year or so, anyway. Maybe permanently if it works out."

Ryle whistled through his teeth. "Think you're up to the challenge?"

"I'd darn well better be. The boat has sailed. It's too late to change my mind."

"It'll be a boost for the town having you here."

"You mean it'll be a boost for the tourist trade?" When his eyebrow peaked, she raised one of her own. "St. Joseph had Jesse James. Now Council Grove has Tracy Whelan."

"I'd say you're exaggerating your own importance."

"I have a tendency to do that." And, she thought, a tendency to say something sarcastic whenever anyone mentioned Council Grove.

"Let people talk if they will. They'll get over it," Ryle told her.

"I just don't want Michael to be hurt."

"The kid looks as if he can take it."

On the other side of the swings and slides, Michael was rolling on the grass and laughing as the dog tried its best to lick his face.

"Looks can be deceiving," Tracy said. She waited, hoping Ryle would say something about wanting to see her again. Was he married? Probably. But maybe not. He wasn't wearing a wedding ring.

A loud beep sounded, startling her, before she realized that he had one of those pocket gadgets to announce emergency calls. Her father had carried one, too.

He combed his fingers through his hair. "Gotta go. Be seeing you, Whelan."

"Right, Tanner." Was that it?

She watched as he walked across the street and climbed into his dusty station wagon. He paused before driving away and touched a hand to his forehead in a kind of salute. The smile he gave her answered her question. Tanner hadn't changed. He wasn't a man to send out signals if he didn't mean them. And that smile was a signal, without a doubt. She'd be seeing him.

All at once it seemed as if everything would be all right. She had one friend. Two, counting Leigh. What more did anyone need?

"Come on, Mikey," she called.

"Not yet."

"Now." She held firm. "We're already a whole day later than we were supposed to be." She lifted a restraining hand as he automatically sprang to the defensive, protesting that it wasn't his fault. "I'm not blaming *you,* Mikey. It's *my* fault. I was stumbling around in a mental fog all week and it took me longer to get everything done than it should have. Now, let's stop arguing and get a move on, okay? Before Leigh sends out the highway patrol looking for us."

"Don't call me Mikey," he grumbled as he crawled into the back seat of the car with Willie.

"Sorry."

"It makes me sound like a baby."

"I know. I forgot."

Turning right on Main Street, she followed it to Creek Road. Then she turned left and continued until it curved out of town. The houses slid farther back from the road and the distances between them stretched wider.

Willows dipped their branches so low in places that a person walking would have had to duck to avoid them. She inhaled deeply, breathing in the sharply familiar smell of this place. It was actually a mingling of smells—the willows in their damp earth, the wildflowers that bloomed in such profusion, the breeze blowing off the lake. Until now, she'd never noticed how vividly smells could evoke certain memories. She hadn't been back in ten years, yet the instant she caught that fleeting scent, her whole life here—Leigh, Scott, Ryle, everything—flashed through her mind, fresh and whole.

"How far are we going to be living from civilization?" Michael whined. "This gets worse and worse."

"It's only a couple of miles. There's an old bike in the garage at the stables—unless it's been thrown out. You can bicycle wherever you want to go."

He groaned and sank down in the seat with his eyes shut.

"You'll like it. Trust me."

"I'm still hungry."

"You're always hungry."

There it was. Tracy's mouth went dry as the house and stables loomed into sight. Leigh was on the porch. Tall and wide-hipped, in baggy jeans. Angular and scrub-faced, her fiery-red hair pulled back severely with a rubber band. She waved both arms wildly as if she were attempting to flag down a runaway train.

Michael caught sight of her and groaned again.

"You'll like her."

"Trust me," they said together.

"YOU LOOK LIKE DEATH," Leigh told her over tall glasses of iced tea, after Michael had gone out to see the horses.

"Thanks."

"It's predictable. It's a well-known fact that hairdressers never do anything right with their own hair."

"You read that in *Reader's Digest*, I presume?"

"Tell me about Kansas City." Leigh put her elbows on the table, rested her chin on her hands and waited.

"All about it?"

"Everything. It must have been pretty hard to leave an exciting metropolis for Hicktown, USA, but I'm glad you did. I've always felt that this was your real home—and besides, I need you here. Oh, Trace, you're more beautiful than ever."

"You said I looked like death."

"You do. But you make a beautiful corpse. Why did I have to choose a best friend who'd make Helen of Troy look like the Bride of Frankenstein?"

"You're talking perfect nonsense."

Nothing had changed. It was as if the two had been together just yesterday, though they hadn't seen each other in years.

Leigh wasn't comfortable away from the town and its surrounding area; the small city of Moberly, about 30 miles distant, was the farthest she'd ever traveled, with the sole exception of her trip to Kansas City, and that was for Tracy's father's funeral. She'd taken the bus and returned to Council Grove almost immediately afterward. She'd once confided to Tracy that she just didn't feel like herself, Leigh Monahan, anywhere but at home. So that's where she stayed and Tracy had long since accepted it. But all these years, they'd written to each other, and occasionally, during especially difficult or depressing times, they'd indulged in lengthy telephone calls.

Leigh suddenly slapped her hands down on the table, grinning widely. "You haven't said a word about the way *I* look."

"You look exactly the same."

"That, Trace, is not a compliment." She leaped up and pirouetted away from the table, then posed, beauty-contest-style with a flourish of one hand. "Look closer. Don't you see it?"

"Give me a hint. What am I supposed to be seeing?"

"There's a man in my life."

"Oh." Tracy smiled. There had always been a man in Leigh's life. But never the same one for long. Two dates. Three. Four, tops. Then he looked elsewhere.

"I guess I come on too strong," she'd say, as philosophically as her shattered heart would allow. "But what the heck? I gotta be me."

The screen door slammed open and Michael skipped into the kitchen with Willie at his heels. "Those horses are neato! That guy, Ed, says I can ride the new pony tomorrow. If it's okay with you, Leigh."

"Sure. No reason why not."

"I like her. But she's a weird color."

Leigh sniffed, pretending to feel insulted. "She's a buckskin and I think she's beautiful. She's my very favorite."

"I like the shiny black with the white legs."

"That's Roxy. You've got a good eye for horseflesh, Bucko. She's a little more tricky. But you'll be taking her through her paces by this time next week."

"No kidding?"

"Leigh!" Tracy kept her voice even, not wanting to be a wet blanket. Still, her friend's promise had been too rash to ignore. "He can't ride. He's never even been on a pony before."

"What kind of sister are you?" Leigh shot back, winking at Michael. "Leaving out the most vital part of the boy's education. We'll make up for it though, won't we, Mikey?"

"Neat-o!" Incredible as it was, the boy didn't correct her use of the hated nickname or even attempt to struggle out of reach when Leigh tousled his hair. He opened the refrigerator door.

"What do you think you're doing?" Tracy asked.

"Getting some lemonade."

"Don't you think you should ask?"

"He doesn't have to, Trace," Leigh answered for him. "This is his home now, too."

Tracy cringed but let it pass. She felt relieved to see her brother settling in so easily. But it was going to be a gargantuan job keeping him in line, especially now that he had Leigh for an ally.

"Ed says you'd better get a move on if you're gonna get to Moberly on time," Michael said, sliding onto one of the kitchen chairs with his lemonade. "Wherever Moberly is."

"Oops." Leigh looked at her watch. "I almost forgot."

"You have to leave?" Tracy asked.

"You know my folks have been living in Moberly since Dad retired, right?"

"Of course. You wrote me about it."

"Well, one of my cousins is in from Texas with his new bride and Mom's having a big barbecue to celebrate. I promised weeks ago I'd attend." She clapped a hand to her mouth. "Didn't I tell you?"

"No...but it's all right," Tracy said, working hard to hide her disappointment.

"I would have canceled, but you were supposed to arrive yesterday morning and I thought we'd have plenty of time to visit."

"I know. It took me a lot longer to get organized than I expected. Getting packed, closing up mother's house for the summer, storing my own stuff..."

Leigh chewed her bottom lip as she listened. "Why don't I just call and beg off?"

"Don't do that. Please."

"You're sure? My mom's big on family get-togethers, or I'd— Wait. I know." Her voice grew louder as it always did when she was excited. "You and Mikey come along. There'll be loads of kids for him to play with and my folks would love to see you again."

Tracy sighed. "No. I really don't feel up to it. But thanks. Maybe next time."

"Can I go, Trace. Please?" Michael wiped his mouth with the back of his hand. "I want to play with some other kids and—"

Tracy was astonished that her brother would even consider visiting with strangers. It was completely unlike him. "I don't think so," she said, interrupting his rush of words. "Leigh will have enough to do without looking after you."

"You'll have to bring your PJs," Leigh told him, as if she hadn't heard Tracy's objections. "I'm planning to stay overnight. I've got some shopping I want to do in the morning. I don't get to Moberly all that often, so I like to take advantage of the stores whenever I go."

"I don't think—"

"Come on, Trace," Leigh broke in with a touch of impatience. "He won't be in the way. There will be lots of other kids, so he'll have a great time, and besides, I'd love his company for the drive. Maybe with some free hours you can zip into town and have a look-see at your very own shop. Consider its possibilities—or lack of them."

"I *would* like to see it."

"Then that's settled. Move it, Mikey." Leigh gave him a playful shove. "Get your overnight things."

"Neat-o!" Michael squealed as he raced into the other room.

Tracy shook her head. "He doesn't usually take to adults that fast."

"Little boys like me. I repeat. *Little* boys."

"Stop putting yourself down and tell me about this new man in your life." Tracy knew her friend was dying to talk about him and only wanted to be coaxed. "You've never mentioned him before."

"I'm trying a whole new tack with this one." Leigh touched a finger to her lips. "I don't brag about him, or say how smart he is, or how good-looking. That way, I fool the fates. You see?"

Tracy laughed. "No. I don't see."

"I don't want them to know how much I like him, or they might decide to take him away."

"He sounds special."

"He is. Oh, Trace. He's so incredibly—" She caught herself just in time and paused. "So incredibly average." She feigned a yawn. "You might even remember him from the old days. But you'll see for yourself. He's coming to the barn dance."

"Barn dance? You have to be kidding."

"I wrote you about it, muddle head. For the stables' grand reopening. We've been semiclosed since Dad retired and handed the reins over to me—no pun intended. As you may have noticed, I—or rather, we—did some remodeling. And we bought a few more horses, too."

"'We'? Oh, you mean Ed Collins. Your new partner. Now there's a man you actually *did* mention to me."

Leigh grinned. "Yeah, my new partner—and former employee. I guess you haven't met him yet, but he's been working here as a stable hand for, oh, six years. He's got a room in town but he spends almost all his time here. Anyway, last winter, when I thought I'd have to declare bankruptcy—remember?—Ed offered to invest his savings in the business. Sure surprised me; Ed's such a shy quiet type you hardly ever know what he's thinking."

Tracy nodded. "So, thanks to Ed, the Monahan stables is out of debt for the first time in recorded history."

"Yup. Ed handles the finances now and he does a better job than I ever did—or my dad, either. It's funny, I've never seen Ed so...excited before. Even this barn dance is his idea. There'll be fiddlers, callers, Japanese lanterns. Men in high-heeled boots and ten-gallon hats. Women in swirling skirts. All that good ol' corny stuff."

"Sounds super."

"It'll give you a chance to see people again."

"That part doesn't sound so super."

"Maybe not. But you're in for a big surprise here, my bashful little friend, if you think I'm going to let you hide your pretty head under a hair dryer. I'm going to see that you get back into life with a capital *L*."

"Ready!" Michael announced, waving his pajamas. "They were at the very bottom of my suitcase."

"Where's your toothbrush?"

"In my pocket. Are we going or aren't we, Leigh?" He twisted out of reach before Tracy could collect a hug. "Race you to the truck."

"Your shop keys are in the envelope on top of the fridge," Leigh called, tearing after him.

"Don't worry about me," Tracy muttered, as she watched the two drive away. "I'll be fine."

It felt strange with Michael gone. But Leigh was right. The shop could be better investigated without a restless nine-year-old underfoot.

The shop. Her shop. She could hardly wait to see it.

CHAPTER TWO

THERE WERE THREE ROOMS, two of which might have been more properly called cubbyholes. The show window was grimy and the floor tiles were a stomach-churning shade of lime green. The walls were so filthy it was difficult to tell what their original color was. It didn't matter. They would soon be oyster white. And the outdated equipment would eventually be replaced. Ditto the plumbing. But for now a thorough scrubbing would have to suffice.

Tracy turned on all the lights and went outside to view the shop from the street. It was hers, and that alone made it beautiful. The tremendous amount of work it required would be pure joy.

She had to remind herself of that quite a few times over the next two hours, as she swept and mopped and scoured. She was on her hands and knees scrubbing the bathroom floor when she heard a loud knock on the shop window.

"Are you in there, Whelan?"

"I'm here," she answered, recognizing Ryle's voice. She pushed up her sleeves and got to her feet. Rivulets of dirty scrub water made gray streaks down her arms. Great. She looked even more disheveled than she had when she'd met him at the restaurant. "To what do I owe this visit?"

"Maybe I'm the Welcome Wagon."

"With the tar and feathers."

He didn't smile. Instead he reached out to brush a stray lock of hair from her eyes. "How can you expect people to forget the past if *you* can't? People forgive. And there are some good people in this town."

She caught her lower lip between her teeth. "I don't care to be forgiven for something I didn't do."

"And you came back to prove your innocence?"

"I came back to prove that I don't give a damn what your good people think." Her hair flopped back over her forehead again.

For some reason, he thought it was funny. He shook his head and grinned. "You say 'damn' like a little kid who's using the word for the first time and feeling terribly grown-up about it."

"I've used the word before, believe me."

"Besides, you *do* care what people think, or you wouldn't get so hot and bothered about it."

"Okay, I do." She inhaled deeply. "If you've come for a shampoo and set, I'm not open for business yet."

He gave her a sharp look. He'd never understood her impulse to turn everything into a joke whenever she was nervous or upset. "Where are Michael and the mutt?"

"Michael's in Moberly with Leigh. Willie is home, lounging on the porch, recuperating from what I did to him." She grimaced. "Just what was it you wanted?"

"It happens I have some free time. I thought I'd offer a hand to the new lady in town. Is there something I can do?"

"Is there something you can do? Can you even ask that with a straight face? Tanner, if you came to offer help as a token gesture and you're expecting me to refuse, roll up your sleeves. You're out of luck. How are you at unclogging sinks? I have three that need attention."

"Three." He whistled through his teeth. "I'll give it a try. Got a garden hose?"

She jerked a thumb over her shoulder. "In the alley."

"Tell you what." He slowly stroked his chin and narrowed one eye. "We'll work, say, three hours. Then we'll call it quits. We'll go home, clean up and I'll take you out to dinner."

She shook her head. "I can't take time out to eat."

"If I hadn't come, it would take you six hours to do the same work, mathematically speaking. Not taking into consideration that I probably work faster. So it's work and dinner—or so long, Tanner."

"Work and dinner," she agreed, secretly pleased that he'd given her the ultimatum. "*If* you let me pay."

He rubbed the fingers of one hand against the leg of his jeans, an impatient gesture she remembered. "Is that how it's done in Kansas City?"

"Yes." She put on her most determined face. "And in Omaha, Nebraska, and Amarillo, Texas. When someone does you a favor, you repay."

"Hmm." He stuck out his tempting lower lip and looked past her out the window. "You'll have to be patient with an old-fashioned country boy like me, Whelan. I pay tonight, or it's no deal. Next time, maybe, we'll toss for it."

She considered the state of her sinks and the prospect of seeing him walk out the door. He wasn't bluffing. "You're on."

"Good."

Then it struck her. "What do you mean you work faster?"

But Ryle only grinned, a familiar, maddening grin, as he rolled up his shirt-sleeves and set to work.

He whistled tunelessly as he wielded plunger and hose, and Tracy hummed along when the melody was recognizable. Twice he had to leave and drive home to pick up tools, a wrench and a snake. But before the three-hour deadline was reached, the sinks were free flowing. The floors were washed and one long wall was clean and ready for painting.

Peeling off her rubber gloves, Tracy sighed and looked around. "The more work I do, the more I see that needs doing. Guess I'll tackle the showroom walls after dinner."

"Nope." Ryle folded his arms across his chest. "There won't be any 'after.' Dinner will take the rest of the evening."

"Where were you planning to take me? San Francisco?"

"I don't like to bolt my food."

"Bolt your food? You could eat blindfolded and with chopsticks and still have hours to spare."

"Humor me, just this once? For old times' sake."

So it was home for a soak and a change of clothes. Not too long a soak though; they had synchronized their watches and Ryle had given her exactly one hour. After a few minutes of indecision, she chose her sleeveless beige summer cotton with its full skirt and semifitted bodice, which showed the slim line of her figure to better advantage. Up until now, he had seen her only in the shapeless, fatigues-style work clothes that would have defied a professional weight guesser.

A pair of beige string sandals completed her outfit and a necklace of apple-green beads added a touch of color. She brushed her hastily shampooed and blow-dried hair until it gleamed, then fastened it into a satiny loop atop her head with a matching green clip.

Ryle was at the door right on schedule and watched, fascinated, as she stood before the hall mirror applying her lip gloss. Then, to hide a sudden feeling of shyness, she smoothed her skirt and swung her bag briskly over her shoulder.

He had gone to a bit of trouble to impress her, too, she noticed. He'd hosed off his station wagon and even cleared some of the clutter out of the back seat.

A vet must have to do a lot of lifting, she thought, her eyes running up and down the length of him as casually as she could manage. His shoulders and arms displayed their strong muscular development even in the loose casual cut of his sports coat, and his cream-colored shirt was open at the throat, just enough to show a glimpse of a metallic ornament—a cross, a medallion?—that nestled against the amber-colored hair on his chest.

There was something irresistibly sexy about the fresh-from-the-shower look of his hair, darker when it was damp.

And about the faint smell of his shaving lotion. Shaving lotion he'd applied thinking of her?

Down, Tracy, she scolded herself.

"Is something wrong?" he asked, puzzled, when he'd turned the key in the ignition.

"I was thinking how spiffy you look tonight," she said, deciding to be at least halfway honest. Men liked compliments just as much as women did.

"Spiffy. Is that good or bad?"

"It means you look distinguished and frightfully handsome."

His face reddened. "Shouldn't I be the one to compliment you on how you look in that dress?"

"Are there rules about such things in Council Grove?"

"Definitely."

"Go ahead then. You think I look spiffy?"

"You look..." He pushed his foot down on the gas pedal and straightened his arms on the steering wheel. "You know damned well how delectable you look."

Delectable. That was better than spiffy, wasn't it? And even more promising. "May I consider that a compliment?"

"Consider it anything you please."

There it was again. A definite hint of hostility. She'd felt it earlier, at the restaurant—when she'd told him she was back in Council Grove to stay. She'd brushed it aside then, but wasn't sure how to respond now, whether to ignore his coolness or confront it.

"Do you remember my grandfather?" she finally asked, deciding to lead their conversation to safer ground. "He loved this part of the country. And do you remember that fifteen-year-old Chevy of his, with one side so caved in the door wouldn't open?"

"I remember."

"He was always talking about taking me on a long trip. We'd see Meremac Caverns, Hannibal, Lake of the Ozarks. We'd hit every town in the state with a population over sixteen, he said. Then we'd know we'd been somewhere. It was never more than a dream, though. He was outside pushing as often as he rode. The car could hardly be trusted for a trip to the supermarket.''

"That heap looked like a luxury limo compared to the one I drove," Ryle said. "I took my life in my hands every time I rode in it.''

"I don't recall your even having a car. Didn't we have to use your dad's?''

"The car was after your time." His laugh sounded gravelly. "For a while, I used to mark off my days that way. Everything was either 'before Tracy' or 'after Tracy.'''

His surprising confession silenced her for most of the next mile. She thought of several things she might say to him, then decided to let his comment pass. Mentally she kicked herself for sitting so close to the window—and so far away from Ryle—when she'd got into the car. Now it would be too obvious if she slid over, unless she got an invitation, which didn't seem likely.

"Granddad used to tell me," she went on, "'You can have your Paris and your Rome. I'll take Missouri anytime. It has scenery, history, everything.'''

"That's because he was born right here," said Ryle, "and his family—your family—goes back for generations in this area. Your grandfather had a special feeling for the land of his people." His voice was unusually solemn. "Like the Indians do.''

Tracy smiled. Ryle was proud of his Blackfoot ancestry. His Indian blood was apparent not only in the color of his eyes but the strength of his pride. Even as a teenager, he'd been well versed in Indian mythology, customs and lore; he'd spent hours talking with her grandfather, swapping stories and exchanging information. They'd shared a sense of passionate concern and indignation about the fate of the Indians, as well as a deep fascination with their traditional way of life. Shortly before he died, her grandfather had given Ryle some beaded jewelry and a few old photographs of a Blackfoot encampment, things he'd inherited from his own father. She hadn't thought about that in years.

"Do you still have those old pictures he gave you?" she asked suddenly.

His calm, unwavering gaze met hers. "I would never let anything happen to them. You know that."

"Right." She felt better now. Whatever had triggered his contrary mood, it had lifted. There was a new warmth in his voice and in his eyes, kindled by memories of her grandfather. They spent the next few minutes in companionable silence, then Ryle pulled an Indian story out of his storehouse of tepee tales, and she listened with an air of exaggerated gravity as she used to. Did people ever change? Ryle hadn't, and she was glad.

"Do you like fish?" he asked, with an out-of-left-field change of subject.

"Fish?" She considered a white lie. Something told her that fish was to be on their menu that night. "It isn't my favorite," she admitted.

"You'll like this."

I'll like anything, Ryle Tanner, she thought, as long as I can eat it sitting across the table from you again.

The *Ozark Queen* was a converted trawler that looked as if it might have been built during the Great Depression. The rough, unpainted boards were unceremoniously draped with fish netting. The boat sat near the lake's edge, and they had to cross a rickety plank to reach the entrance.

Inside, though, the restaurant was clean, cozy and much larger than would be supposed viewing it from the road. It was also crowded, and since Ryle insisted on a table overlooking the water, they had a long wait. It didn't matter. They had so much to talk about that time flew by.

When they were finally seated, Tracy found she was ravenous. She ate with complete enjoyment, wholly concentrated on her meal of perfectly cooked and seasoned "catch of the day," and didn't look up until she heard Ryle clearing his throat.

"The leaves in the middle are painted on the plate," he told her gravely. "I was afraid you might try to eat them, too."

She dabbed at her lips with a napkin and smiled. "This was delicious. There's a secret to frying fish and I never learned it. Mine turns out more scrambled than fried. In Home Ec class they taught us how to make floating islands and prune whip, but nothing really substantial."

An attractive woman in a red dress entered to a sprinkle of applause and sat at the piano. She wiggled her fingers at Ryle before beginning to play "Moon River." He nodded and grinned at her.

Tracy felt an uncharacteristic twinge of jealousy. Did he come here often? And if he did, who did he come with? Had he ever dated the pianist? Had there been anything serious between them? She took a sip of water to disguise the giggle that started low in her throat when she considered her own nonsense. Had she expected him to dine alone all those years they'd been apart?

Later, as they strolled along the lake, they spoke very little. The light from the moon rippled on the water, and seemed to touch it with silver. From somewhere in the trees above them came the song of a mockingbird. Faint music rose from a boat-rental dock farther along the shore. In the distance, little boats flitted like lightning bugs.

She'd never noticed the *Ozark Queen* before, perhaps because of its unassuming weather-beaten appearance. But she remembered the boats and she wondered if Ryle was remembering them, too. Their first kiss had taken place in one of those boats. It had been the first real kiss she'd ever received from a boy and she'd all but fallen overboard from the impact. It hadn't been a hard, demanding kiss. It had been brief and tender. Yet that kiss had hit her with the force of a lightning bolt, and she'd never forgotten it.

There had been many other times for them and many other kisses. She remembered especially their last night together. They had rented a little boat with *Melanie* painted on the side, set down their oars when they were a distance from the shore, and looked at the stars as if those stars were shining only for them. Ryle had brushed his lips against her hair and told her how good she smelled. Their kisses grew more urgent. Raw heat emanated from his body and his forehead was shiny with perspiration.

"What am I going to do about you?" he'd asked against her ear as delicious shivers of discovery zigzagged down her spine. His breathing was uneven and his lips trembled as they took hers. Her heart might have been a rocket soaring above them.

Until then, she'd only dreamed of how it could be between two people. She was overwhelmed by the fierceness of his yearning and no less overwhelmed by her own desire. In those moments, she'd experienced an excitement that was entirely new to her and she'd known she would never, ever tire of being in his arms.

But then he'd released her, and she could still recall what he'd said. "You don't appreciate how strong I am, Tracy." When she hadn't understood, he'd quietly added, "Maybe someday you will."

Someday. It had been so long ago. They'd been so young. She had kissed other men since, but she'd always remembered Ryle and the special way he'd made her feel.

"I'm glad you've come back, Whelan," he said now, his voice hushed and quiet.

"I'm glad too."

"I wasn't sure I'd forgiven you."

"Forgiven me for what?"

"For walking out on me."

Was he teasing? "The question is, who walked out on who? Or is it whom?"

"Don't be flip with me, Tracy. I'd say the one who refused the phone calls and took up with someone else is the one who did the walking."

"You never had time for me. I didn't think you cared."

"I cared."

"How was I supposed to know?"

He stopped walking and faced her. He wasn't teasing. He was serious. "Why in hell did you think I was hitting the books so hard? I thought it was for us—our future."

She could feel the blood heating in her veins, could feel her lips throbbing. They stared at each other for a moment. His eyes glittered, though with anger or with passion she couldn't tell. Was he going to kiss her—or shake her senseless? "You should have told me," she finally said.

"What good would it have done? What chance did I have against a Barclay?"

"You could have put up a fight."

"Is that what you wanted? A fight?" He gripped her shoulders, and off balance, she thudded against him.

"Not exactly," she answered, with a sharp intake of breath. "But at least it would have shown that I mattered to you."

An intense fire lit up his eyes. His skin looked very tanned in the moonlight. For an instant she could imagine him as a fierce Indian brave in war paint, ready to do battle.

"What did you want? I couldn't write poetry and I couldn't afford flowers."

"I wanted the words. They wouldn't have cost anything."

"Maybe I didn't know the right ones."

You know them now, she thought, tensing for the kiss she needed. The kiss she knew would come.

"There's unfinished business between us, Whelan," he murmured, hardly moving his lips.

"I know," she breathed, not daring to move.

An eerie, trembling call rose from the darkness and he pointed. "An owl."

"Don't Indians consider the sighting of an owl at night a sign of impending disaster? You told me that once."

"And it was true, wasn't it," he said almost bitterly, pulling his eyes from her mouth. "We'd better go. It's getting late."

That was it? She wanted to hurl aside the arm he offered.

"I've heard of grudges, but this is ridiculous," she said under her breath when they'd started back. "All these years."

"I happen to have a long memory." A corner of his mouth lifted slightly in a telltale smile.

"So what does it take to make you forget?"

"I'll have to think about it."

"We can at least have some music." She reached for the radio switch.

"No." He caught her hand. "It would interfere with the thought transference that exists between us."

"With the kind of thoughts I'm getting from you, we can do with a little interference."

"Not only that, the radio doesn't work."

"Some sense of humor you have," she said, looking at him sideways.

As the headlights slid across the side of the house Willie barked his welcome. Where had the hours gone? Tracy saw the dog's face at the back window before the lights went out and it was dark again. Then the engine was still.

"It's not very late," she said, glancing at the dashboard clock. "Would you like to come in?"

She pictured herself fixing coffee, with him sitting at the kitchen table, watching. After a while, he would loosen up and agree to make allowances for their ages at the time of their doomed "love affair." Everything would be all right again.

His eyes caressed her face as he shifted toward her and slid his arm across the back of the car seat. Her lips parted without volition. "I can't," he said. "I promised the Judsons I'd look in on their goat before I called it a night."

"Their goat," she echoed tonelessly.

All those years ago it had been homework. Now it was a goat.

"Thanks for tonight, Ryle." She was tired. More tired than she'd realized. The long drive and then the work at the shop had taken a lot out of her. "I really enjoyed it."

"Do you want me to walk you to the door?"

Not if you have to ask, you dope.

"It isn't necessary," she said. "Someone—Ed Collins, I guess—is still up working. I saw the light near the barn as we drove by. I'll be okay. You'd better hurry over to see your goat."

If he heard the sarcasm in her voice, he didn't let on. "Right."

"Good night, then."

Welcome back to Council Grove, Tracy, she thought grimly, as she trudged up the gravel path to the house. That was what their dinner had been all about. That, and the opportunity to remind her of past sins, in case she'd forgotten. Now he'd finally had his chance to say it and he could get on with his life again.

"Tracy!"

He was out of the car before she could turn to ask what he wanted. His arms wound around her with increasing strength, to trap her against him, her arms at her sides. His lips opened, warm and confident, over hers before she could register surprise. It was a kiss to explode a lifetime's memory of kisses and begin a new one. A kiss that could only laugh at her previous fantasies.

It might have sent her reeling if he hadn't held her fast. His lips, his tongue, his teeth, all came into play, moving, twisting, coaxing, demanding that she give more, more and still more to this first reunion of their shared desires. Bold fingers kneaded her back as he drank in her sweetness and filled her eager mouth with the taste of him.

When he released her, she reached for the gatepost to hold herself steady. "Be ready at five tomorrow afternoon," he said, smiling down at her with a smile that was glazed with passion. "We'll have a cookout."

How could she possibly go with him? There was far too much to be done getting the shop ready. And there was Michael, who would be back by then. No, it was too soon, much too soon.

"Five," she heard herself repeating. "Unless the Judson goat needs you."

The gate made a familiar scritching sound as it moved against its leaning frame. It was a sound that brought back more of the past. In the old days, Leigh's mother always used to say they'd get it fixed. But they never did. That gate announced visitors as surely as a doorbell and everyone would gather round to see who was coming—friend or bill collector.

"Miz Whelan?" A dark shape loomed up between the house and the outbuildings. "Name's Ed Collins. Hope I won't disturb you with my hammering. Leigh thinks we should get these new feeders built tonight."

"Hello, Ed. Nice to finally meet you. I've heard a lot about you, how great you are with horses, and..." Her voice trailed off in embarrassment as Ed just stood there, stonily silent, totally unresponsive to her friendly chatter. "Don't worry about the noise," she said quickly. "I'm so tired I could sleep inside a bass drum."

This, then, was the Ed Collins who'd saved Leigh from bankruptcy. Her new partner. Tracy gave him an appraising look. He was tall and very lean, with a shambling walk and a hard-to-read face—and she suspected that his face wouldn't be much more revealing in the light of day. She felt instinctively that he disapproved of her, but at the moment she was too exhausted to care. Or even to wonder why.

"Was that Doc Tanner with you?" he asked.

"Yes, it was."

"I thought so." Another question flicked in his eyes, but he turned away without asking it. "Good night."

"Good night."

From the front porch where she stood, she could see the black, hulking shape of Soapstone Hill. She could see the roof of the Fletcher farmhouse, too, though it was nearly half a mile away. Rebuilt now, it had been the site of a fire more than ten years ago...

The first of the fires. The sky that night had been so lit up that people had come from miles around. Leigh and Tracy had stood huddled together watching, when Tracy saw Scott Barclay standing alone—away from the others. His eyes were round with wonder.

"Did you ever see so many pretty shades of red and orange?" he'd asked. "All different. Look. If you stare into it hard enough, you can see a face. Right in the middle of the flames."

Tracy had seen nothing pretty about the blaze. It was horrifying. A couple of people said they'd seen a tramp in the neighborhood earlier. Maybe he'd been sleeping in the barn and dropped a cigarette in the hay.

"He could be inside," Tracy had whispered, awestruck. "He wouldn't have a chance."

"Nobody's in there," Scott had assured her.

"There might be. The tramp who started the fire."

"Don't worry," he'd insisted. "The place was empty."

She didn't know why then, but a fist of fear had squeezed her middle.

There were other fires after that. Nine of them over the next eight months. Scott would always be among the first to arrive on the scene and among the last to leave. There'd be excitement in his face that Tracy saw at no other time. The same excitement would come back whenever he talked about the fires, and he talked about them often. Too often.

Then it struck her that these bursts of excitement often came a day or so before the fires. It was as if he knew ahead of time. But that was impossible, she'd thought, unless...

She'd followed him one night to the junior high and caught him as he was about to set his eleventh fire.

"What's it to you," he'd asked, his voice shrill and strange. "Nobody ever gets hurt. And it's the only excitement anybody gets in this burg."

They'd argued and wrestled, making so much noise the custodian heard and turned in an alarm. Enraged because she'd put an end to his furtive pleasures, Scott told the police that Tracy had been an accomplice, that it had all been her idea from the start. Later, when he'd calmed down, he changed his story. But by then, everyone believed that it was Tracy's craving for excitement that had induced him to set the fires. Since they were both under eighteen, they were treated as juveniles. Scott was sent to a hospital for psychological testing and Tracy was released into her parents' custody.

Unable to bear up under the gossip, her mother insisted they move. First it was St. Louis. But her father's prospective business partner backed out of their financial agreement and they soon moved on to Kansas City.

She'd heard from Leigh that Scott spent some time in a psychiatric institution and that when he was finally released, he got involved with drugs. He fell into one scrape after another and was killed two years later when his motorcycle, traveling at top speed, veered off the road and struck a tree.

Poor Scott, Tracy thought. He was nothing like people supposed he was. He'd needed help desperately. But she'd been too young and immature to know what to do. Even after all these years it was hard for her to shake the feeling that she'd let him down. She found that she could now think of Scott without bitterness or blame; her anger was reserved for the others, Ryle's "good people," who'd been so quick to believe the frantic lies of a disturbed boy. So quick to think the worst.

Willie scampered around her, wanting attention, as she let herself into the house. When she'd slipped out of her shoes, she knelt down to rub his soft curly ears, grateful for the distraction that wrenched her out of the painful past.

"A cookout," she said aloud, pondering what Ryle had proposed. "What sort of cookout?" Would there be other people or just the two of them?

Whatever it was, she'd be ready and waiting.

She'd been wrong about her ability to sleep, though. The moon seemed to be brighter in Council Grove than in Kansas City. And it fell directly across her bed. The hammering went on and on, it's rhythms echoing and reechoing in her head.

But it wasn't the noise that finally kept her awake. It was the memory of Ryle, the taste of his kiss and the anticipation of more to come.

CHAPTER THREE

SCRUBBING THE CABINETS and utility closets at the shop took most of the morning, but happy thoughts of the evening to come kept Tracy floating above the soapy water and scrub brush.

The serviceman came to install her telephone at midday, and eager to put her new toy to use, she decided to call Ryle. But before she'd even looked up his listing, there was a loud ring and Leigh was on the line.

"How on earth did you get the number?" Tracy marveled.

"I have my connections, if you'll pardon the pun. And wouldn't it be horrendous, I asked myself, if your first call turned out to be a wrong number?"

"Horrendous," Tracy agreed. Bless Leigh. Who else could possibly understand her bubbly excitement over something so pedestrian as a telephone?

"Besides," Leigh chattered on, hardly taking a breath, "I wanted to tell you I'm staying over another day. There's a horse I might buy and the owner won't be back until tomorrow morning."

"What about Michael?"

"What about him? He's fine. Hit it off with some kids here and he's having a wonderful time."

"I don't know if this is a good idea. Maybe—"

"Don't worry so much. Mikey and I are buddies, remember? We understand each other. Now, how about *you*? Is the shop okay? Is it what you wanted?"

"It's perfect, but—"

"Gotta go, kid. Mom wants me to drive her to the store. See you tomorrow night. Or the morning after if it gets too late and we decide to stay over. Ed has my number here if you need me."

"Stay over? But—" Her protest was wasted on a dial tone.

She shrugged, then quickly flipped through her brand-new telephone directory, searching for Ryle's number.

A tape recording informed her that Dr. Tanner wasn't in the office and asked her to leave a message at the sound of the tone. Always intimidated by such devices, she hung up. It would be easier to wait until evening. She had only a couple of hours to go and more than enough work to fill them.

Ryle arrived early and summoned her, dripping, from a perfumed bath, to answer the door. The cookout was on hold, he said. He had an emergency. Not the Judson goat this time, but the Silverstein cow.

"Why not ride along and keep me company? When I'm finished we can do something."

"But it's going to take me at least twenty minutes to get dressed and dry my hair and—"

"You look fine," he told her, squinting through the crack in the door. "I can spare five minutes while you get ready."

So much for the special hairdo she'd planned to try, and the new shade of eye shadow. A hasty twist and pin-up of her still damp hair, a one-two-three application of mascara and lip gloss, and they were on their way.

A second emergency, a dog whose owner suspected it had been poisoned, came after the first. Both cases had happy endings, with collie and cow resting comfortably. But it was after eleven before Ryle was free.

Exhausted, he asked Tracy to drive and sat with his head resting against the back of the seat and his eyes closed. "I could get used to the luxury of having an assistant," he drawled. "I don't suppose you'd consider the job."

"I'll make a deal with you, doc," she countered. "You come in afternoons and do my comb outs, and I'll make your rounds with you at night."

He opened one eye. "Uh ... no thanks."

"You don't think you could handle it?"

"I know my limitations."

They were both famished, but it was too late to do anything but stop at a roadside café for burgers and fries. It was his third straight night of emergency calls, and he wasn't in any condition for polite conversation.

Laughably, it was like the old days; he'd stay up half the night studying, and then the next evening he'd be on the verge of falling asleep. So Tracy would end up doing all the talking—just as she was now. She didn't mind, though. It made her feel relaxed and comfortable.

"Sorry about the way things turned out tonight," he said as he walked her to the gate over her protests that he needn't bother. Roping his long arms around her, he drew her close and administered a kiss that curled her toes in spite of its matter-of-fact delivery. "Want to give me another chance? Tomorrow night? Same time? We'll have another try at our cookout."

"Same time," she murmured, not really caring where they went or what they did.

BUT THE NEXT NIGHT they were in luck. They actually made it to the car and then all the way to Ryle's place without hearing from the beeper even once.

Tracy hadn't felt so lighthearted in years. That whole day, as she scrubbed and scoured the shop walls, she'd bubbled with delicious anticipation. And now she was free. Leigh had called to say that she and Michael wouldn't be back until morning; for the next few hours, she didn't have to worry about her brother's problems, or her friend's, or the state of the shop. This one night was hers—hers and Ryle's.

He was eager to have her meet his "family," and as soon as they left the car, he caught her hand lightly in his and led her to the stables. The instant she saw the beautiful chestnut horse in the first stall, Tracy burst out, "Oh, Ryle, he's magnificent!" The horse's nostrils spread and his head snapped up at the sound of her voice. "But he seems edgy."

"He may never be entirely trusting," Ryle told her grimly, moving closer and speaking softly to reassure the animal.

"What's his name?"

"Mikapi. After a heroic chief of long ago. Brother-of-the-Bear."

"I wonder how I knew it would be something like that?"

Ryle only smiled. "He's really kind of a hero himself, this fellow. I can't talk about the conditions of the place where he was found. I get so incensed I could go back there and . . ." He raised one hand and moved it back and forth, symbolically erasing a thought too hideous to be voiced. "I'll show you the 'before' and 'after' pictures sometime. You wouldn't believe it's the same horse."

Most of Ryle's animals had been rescued from cruel or uncaring homes. There was an adorable pit bull who'd been beaten nearly to death by his master because he didn't have the heart to fight. There was a skeletal shepherd with a limp, who could only qualify for the 'before' pictures as yet, along with a scrawny mother cat and two kittens, two rabbits, another horse and a handful of chickens.

"How do you find time to tend to your menagerie?" she asked.

"A boy half a mile down the road comes in and helps. I use him for a handler, too. He'll probably be a vet someday. There are some terrific kids in this town. I get a group of them together a couple of times a month. It's pretty informal. We fish, camp out, whittle, sing, tell stories. I hope I can instill my love of the outdoors in them. The love Dad instilled in me. Let them know there's more to life than staring at the screen of a video game. It's tragic how many of them don't have fathers."

"There's so much divorce these days," Tracy said, thinking of the problems her mother and stepfather had been having in their marriage. Their blowups, their near breakups, Michael's deliberate attempts to cause trouble between them, and at the same time, the unhappiness that trouble seemed to bring him.

"I'm not talking about divorce. It's funny. But more times than not, a father gives more of himself to his kids after a separation. He has his visitation rights spelled out and he uses them. No, I'm talking about fathers who are there—but not *really* there. They've got more important concerns than their children—they think."

There was a moment's silence between them. Then Ryle gently took her arm and urged her toward the house. "Come on in. I know you haven't seen this place in a good ten years, but it hasn't changed—much."

Tracy was almost reluctant to follow him into the house, unprepared for the rush of feeling she knew would come. She drew a deep shuddery breath as she stepped into the living room…and realized with a sudden shock of relief that everything was different. Oh, the house itself was unchanged, but it *felt* completely different. It no longer held his mother's cheerful, orderly presence, with the neat rows of flowering plants that Tracy remembered, and the gleaming polished furniture and the bright chintz curtains. Tracy had to grin. The house reflected Ryle now, Ryle alone.

In spite of his precision about time, he had always been remarkably disorganized when it came to his surroundings. Even back in their high school days, his room had been a permanent shambles, with books and clothes strewn recklessly around. Now the whole house looked that way.

Tracy surveyed the small, incredibly cluttered living room, her gaze resting momentarily on a cleared space in the middle of the crowded coffee table. There, she recognized her grandfather's beaded jewelry and one of his Indian photographs, now framed and carefully propped against a large medical dictionary. She smiled to herself, then resumed her inspection of the mess. "What, no TV?" she asked in mock horror.

"Sure, I have my vices." He pointed and Tracy giggled. She hadn't seen it amid the stack of books, boxes and mounds of discarded clothing. She remembered how exasperated she used to get with his hopeless housekeeping. How she and his mother would laughingly threaten to clean up his room so he could find his way out in the mornings. At this very moment, she itched to pile up magazines, sort clothes, straighten shelves...

Ryle's expression told her he'd guessed the road her thoughts were taking. "There's order in this chaos, believe it or not. Everything is exactly where I want it."

"Oh?" With the toe of one sneakered foot, she nudged an unopened utility bill that lay on the floor and looked at him quizzically. "You have a unique filing system."

"Come here." Ryle stepped over a heap of damp towels, muttering something about getting the laundry done. Then he swept newspapers and magazines off the couch and beckoned Tracy to sit down beside him. "Look in that book," he said, pointing at the medical dictionary.

She glanced at him, then gently laid aside the Indian photograph and lifted the heavy book. Inside the cover was a bulging envelope and inside the envelope were pictures. Snapshots taken by Leigh the year she got a camera for her birthday. Photography had turned out to be a short-lived obsession, but that one summer she was forever sneaking up on people to take unflattering candid shots.

There was an embarrassing one of Tracy in rag curlers and a pair of baggy pajamas and another of her on a bicycle, her face red and shiny with sunburn. There was a shot of her and Ryle, sitting on the grass at the high school, their backs to the camera. There was one of Ryle falling asleep over his books and another of the two of them patting a friendly looking dog.

"You've kept them all this time," Tracy said almost inaudibly.

"I've been saving them to start a bonfire. Do you remember this night?" He plucked a picture out of the pile.

It was a group shot taken the night of somebody's birthday party. Tracy and Ryle, their faces blurry, were on opposite sides of the room, each of them talking to someone else—yet they were looking at each other.

"I remember," she said softly, knowing exactly why he'd singled out that particular photograph. It said so much. Their eyes making promises across a crowded room. Promises soon to be broken....

Tracy found herself perilously close to tears. To change the direction of her thoughts, she picked up a small chamois pouch, half-hidden by an old, leather-bound book of Indian myths. She loosened the drawstring and shook two smoothly polished rosy-hued stones into her hand, one stone slightly smaller than the other. "What are these?"

"Ah." He took the larger of the stones and held it between his forefinger and thumb. "These are catlinite. The sacred stone of my people."

She pulled a serious face to match his. "Of *your* people?"

"The Blackfoot."

"Ah. The Blackfoot." She nodded gravely.

"It represents flesh and blood." He uttered the words distinctly, as one might who was revealing a long-kept secret.

"Because of the color?"

"Yes." In the softening light of early evening, Ryle's deepset eyes, tense and shining, hinted at more intimate thoughts. The fan wasn't turned on. The room was close. Warm, moist heat emanated from his body and mingled with hers. He folded her fingers into a fist around the stone, his hand still covering hers. "Because when it's held—so— it's said you can feel its heartbeat. A steady throbbing."

"Oh." Tracy felt the throbbing. But it wasn't coming from the stone.

"In olden times, if a man and woman were deeply in love, they would go out and bury these stones, wrapped tightly together, to the depth of the man's forearm. Of course, it could only be done on the first night of the Spring Moon."

"Of course." Her thoughts whirled about inside her head and without design or consent, her eyes fastened on his mouth. She cleared her throat. "What is a Spring Moon, as opposed to just an ordinary moon?"

"The Spring Moon is what the Blackfoot calls April."

"April first. Ryle, you're making this up."

"You think so? There are many who scoff at things the Blackfoot know to be true." He took the stone from her hand and returned both of them to the pouch.

"What happens once the stones are buried? Do they disappear? Do they turn into gold?"

"No. They become one." He took her wrist, raised it and brushed his lips, hot and moist, across the pulse point, as if he had heard its desperate drumming. "But only... only if the love of the man and woman is true."

Her eyes were pulled to his and her mind caught a picture and held it. A picture of them—her and Ryle—lying together, their bodies touching. Her face burned and she looked down at her other hand, tightly clenched in her lap.

Then Ryle brushed his lips in a rhythmic circle in the center of her open palm and Tracy gasped.

"How long does it take before..." She drew a shaky breath as he kissed each finger lightly. "Before they... become one and the couple can tell if their love is true?"

"Twenty such moons must come and go." As he spoke, his other hand was carrying on an expedition of its own, moving at her waist, finding its way beneath her blouse to sear the bare flesh at the small of her back. As he urged her closer, his other arm went around to encircle her completely, his hand sliding beneath the thin cotton fabric to a place between her shoulder blades.

She tilted her head back and looked at him dizzily. "Twenty months?" she asked, the question echoing inside her mind, though she was barely aware of what they'd been discussing.

"No. Only the first night of each Spring Moon is counted."

"Twenty years?" she tried to refocus her thoughts. "Twenty years is a long time. Isn't..." Her tongue darted out to moisten her parched lips, then darted back to safety again as Ryle's gaze captured it and his grip on her tightened still more. "Isn't there a quicker way to tell?"

"I was hoping you'd ask that," he said thickly.

Making a cradle for her of his arms, he nuzzled her head back still farther and angled his open mouth to better enclose hers. When he withdrew, to allow them breath, his eyes glittered in the half-light.

Tracy was lost. She was only helpless, joyous sensation. Ryle's hands seemed to be everywhere, caressing, touching, and she, too, touched him, needing the closeness, *his* closeness. And then, when it seemed their passion must consume them entirely, Ryle drew away, just enough to reach for her hands and clasp them between their bodies.

"Tracy, Tracy, I want you so badly it hurts—but now is not the time. Not yet."

At her look of surprise and disappointment, he released her hands and moved close again. Wrapping his arms around her, he kissed her forehead, then her eyelids, then the tip of her nose. Moving his hand to stroke her hair, he murmured her name, over and over, as if to assure himself she was really there with him.

Tracy sensed his mood and felt herself relaxing. Yes, it was so right. And they had lots of time.

As their breathing gradually steadied, Ryle tilted back his head, and gave her a faint smile. "Are you hungry?" he asked.

Tracy heard the words, but for a moment they seemed to have no meaning.

"Are you ready for our cookout?" he said.

Cookout. Cookout. Her hold on him relaxed completely, and she sank against the back of the couch. Ryle slowly stood up, then stretched his arms toward her. She placed her hands in his and with barely any effort at all, he pulled her to her feet.

For a moment, they just stood there, fingers still linked, gazing into each other's eyes. Ryle finally freed one hand and raised it to her chin. Tentatively, he slid a rough thumb across her lower lip. No kiss followed. "There are things to be carried, princess. You're going to have to help."

Tracy blinked. "Where are we going?"

"Just outside. Follow me." Leaping over obstacles, he made his way to the kitchen, while she trailed more sedately behind. When she got there, he thrust a large grocery bag and a tightly packed bedroll into her arms.

"What's this for?"

"It makes for more comfortable sitting." He rubbed his backside. "Some of us have less built-in padding than others. There are rocks and brambles to contend with."

"I thought you said we were only going outside."

"We are. Get cracking." He jerked his head toward the back door. "That way. It's closer. I'll get the rest of the things."

Ryle had planned the cookout for his own backyard—the three and a half acres of fields and trees that surrounded the house. Over a wood fire, he pan-fried steaks and roasted ears of corn, while Tracy picked tomatoes from his kitchen garden and cut them into thick slices.

The steaks were cooked to perfection, but Ryle's eager appetite made him careless. In sliding them onto the plates he spattered some of the hot juices down the front of his shirt. As if that wasn't messy enough, he crowned it with a splotch of steak sauce.

"Now I know what to get you for your birthday," Tracy teased. "A bib."

Clucking his tongue in exasperation, he pulled the shirt over his head and slung it carelessly over the branch of a handy dogwood tree.

Tracy's stomach muscles contracted and a tingle began inside her at the sight of his brown, wonderfully formed chest, the scattering of dark amber hair that covered it, and the pattern that hair made as it led the eye down to his tight, low-slung jeans.

"Don't stand on ceremony, Tanner," she threw at him, wanting to make light of her escalating lasciviousness. "Make yourself comfortable."

He grinned. "The same goes for you."

She pressed her lips together and twisted them to one side. "Ahh, no thanks. There's a chill in the air."

The medallion. She willed her greedy eyes to the ornament he wore around his neck. It was crudely made of hammered light metal, probably tin, and was etched with Indian symbols.

"The elements," he told her, noticing where her eyes rested. "Fire, water, earth, air. This was given to me by a young Blackfoot boy a couple of years ago, when I was able to save his dog. It had been hit by a car and for a while things were touch and go. It was my first really difficult case and seeing that animal running on all fours again was all the gratitude I needed. But I wear this to remind myself how good it feels being a vet. At times I need a reminder."

My golden warrior, Tracy thought, not knowing where the phrase came from. Suggested, perhaps, by the orange flames that cast a circle of flickering light around them both. There was a subtle sensuality in eating beside a glowing campfire. But then there was sensuality in everything when she was with Ryle. He'd even had her blushing as she imagined the intimacy between two stones.

A flutter of giddy laughter touched her at the memory and he caught her opened mouth with a kiss, releasing her lips only to draw them in again, until her whole mouth vibrated with new life.

When darkness came, it came quickly, and when the stars appeared, they were close and abundantly sprinkled in the purple night sky. Lazy and contented after their meal and hasty cleanup, Tracy and Ryle sat on the blankets and talked.

"If I could manage it, I'd ride Mikapi up into those hills and camp out about half the time." He pointed in the general direction of the hills, all but vanished now in the darkness. "But I have too many commitments. I can't get away for long. So I have to compromise."

Tracy nodded. "By making your surroundings as much like the wilderness as possible. I like it here."

He had allowed the grasses to grow wild and meadow-like. Dogwood and hawthorne effectively screened the picnic site from the house, from the road, and even from the lights of town. They might actually have been somewhere in the wild, just the two of them.

He told her about Columbia, Missouri, about the university and about the girl he almost married.

"She was a good person," he said. "Times got so tough when I was washing dishes and working as an errand boy and still trying to keep up my grades, I might have junked the whole idea if she hadn't been there, prodding me."

"Why did you decide against marriage?"

"It was a mutual decision. We were very fond of each other, but we both realized that what we felt was the kind of love friends feel—not husband and wife." His voice was low and hesitant and he didn't look at her as he spoke. "If we'd gone through with the marriage, it would have been a mistake. For her and for me. We'd both have lost out on the chance to feel the kind of magic I've felt with you, Tracy." He shrugged one shoulder. "As it turned out, our lives took very different directions. She ended up a big-city vet in California, and I came back here."

"So, did the two of you ever venture out on the first night of the Spring Moon? To bury your catlinite stones?" Tracy tried to sound bright and careless, as though she were tossing off the most casual of questions.

He laughed. "If I'd even suggested such a thing to Meredith, she'd have had me committed. She's a levelheaded type. All logic."

"And what does that make me?"

"Figure it out for yourself." He fastened an arm around her and pressed his lips to the top of her head. "Look up and to your left. There. See those seven stars?"

"I see seven thousand."

"Squint your eyes and use your imagination. They form a fish shape. See it?"

"Maybe." She didn't really. But then she'd never been able to see any Big or Little Dippers when they were pointed out to her, either.

Still, Ryle seemed satisfied with her answer. He launched into a tale about an Indian brave and his beloved, and then he pointed out another grouping of stars and told her the legend of its origin.

Tracy huddled closer to him, warm and content, as he described different constellations and told her the names they'd been given around the long-ago campfires.

The future suddenly looked clear and uncomplicated to her. She and Ryle were together: what else mattered? They were together, sharing the simple beauty of the night sky— a sky unchanged by the passage of ten years or ten thousand.

Tracy began to talk too, slowly at first, about things she'd been reluctant to discuss with anyone before. She talked about the bitter, disillusioning experience of leaving Council Grove, of how her parents had suffered during that time and how her own life had somehow lost its focus. She told him about her own near-attempt at marriage. She'd been feeling depressed and aimless after her father's death, and then she'd met a man who wanted to marry her. She'd let him talk her into it, until she realized that their marriage would have been built on the weak foundations of fantasy.

"I finally figured out what I really wanted was someone to replace my father. To take away the hurt—but only time can do that. And what he wanted was a wife who stayed home and baked bread, whose only problem was how to make white clothes whiter. Thank God I came to my senses before I promised to love, honor, and all that."

While she talked, Ryle listened quietly, without comment or question. Tracy was comforted by his calm silence... and by the way he gently, rhythmically stroked the back of her hand.

After a few minutes, she went on to talk about Michael and how worried she'd been about his manipulative behavior. Resenting his stepfather's intrusion into his life, Michael had learned to antagonize the man when they were alone, then play the little innocent for his mother, setting the two against each other.

"I'll take him on our next overnighter," Ryle promised. "It'll help him to get involved with other boys."

"It might. But remember, he has an iron will. You've been warned."

"I'll carry a two-by-four."

Then she talked about the month of April, the time of the romantic Spring Moon to him, but to her, truly the "cruelest month." The poet was right, she told him. Everything bad that had ever happened to her had happened in April. The trouble in Council Grove and the moving away. Her abandoned marriage plans. Her father's death.

She lapsed into silence, thinking. Remembering. The feelings of despondency that had overtaken her only the previous April had been the biggest reason for her return to face the roots of her depression.

It was in April that she'd begun listening to Leigh's suggestions to "come home," to stop hiding—from herself and from the past. Until then, she hadn't even been able to force herself to drive down on a weekend for a visit with her friend. There was the fact, too, that she'd become increasingly worried about the desperate tone of Leigh's letters and calls after that last failed love affair. Leigh had fallen hard for an attorney who'd come to town to settle the terms of a will. He'd taken her out, wined her and dined her—and then gone back to marry the woman he'd been engaged to all along. Leigh had seemed inconsolable, but her despair had eventually given way to a sad bravado. In each letter, each phone call, she'd begged Tracy to come home. "It'll be the two of us against the world—again," she promised over and over. "Friendship is worth more than love any day."

When Tracy had finally, tentatively, agreed, Leigh immediately set out to find the shop for her, insisting she and Michael live in the house rent free "until you're on your feet, financially speaking."

Now her thoughts began to pick away at the edges of her contentment. Reality emerged. The fire was almost out and there was the smell of rain in the air.

"I'd better be going," she said, stirring.

"Why?"

"It's getting late."

"Does that matter? Your brother is in good hands. Your dog is fed and Ed Collins told me he'd be at the stables tonight."

"If Leigh calls, she'll worry."

"Why should she worry?"

"I don't know, but . . ."

"You aren't going anywhere. We've got some planning to do. To make your next April so terrific that all the others will be overshadowed and forgotten."

Absently she stroked the hand that still held hers. It was tanned and squarish, with blunt fingertips and a callused palm. An ordinary hand. But, oh, what magic it could work.

"How will we do that?" she asked.

"We'll begin tonight."

"Tonight? This is June. You're either two months late or ten months early."

"Let me tell you a story."

"Another tale from the tepee?" She shook her head. "No more tonight."

"All right." He paused, then asked, "What's the date?"

"The third of June. Why?"

"June third," he proclaimed in a solemn voice. "It will henceforth be known as the night you first slept between my blankets."

Her middle vibrated as she laughed. "Do we post this notice on the bulletin board at the town hall?"

"It's posted here. And here," he said, taking one of her hands and pressing it first to his chest, then to hers. "For always."

Gathering new strength, she kissed the hand and put it away with an air of determination. She had to go now, if she intended to go at all. Things were happening too fast. "I think I'll give you a name to go with your ancestry," she said, getting up and brushing pieces of dried grass and leaves from her shorts. "I'll call you He-Who-Tells-Too-Many-Tales."

He caught her ankle and held it while he kissed the back of her knee soundly. "Let me change that to He-Who-Knows-What-He-Needs. And I'll call you She-Who-Runs-Away."

"I suppose that would be fitting," she agreed, pulling free. "Okay, Tanner. Do you want me to help you carry some of this stuff inside? Now or never."

"Never," he said. But recognizing defeat, he got up, too, and began to roll the bedding while Tracy repacked the paper bag with the things that had to be taken back to the house.

"Tomorrow night," Ryle told her between feathery goodnight kisses. "We'll pick up some junk food and take in a movie. There's a couple of old horror flicks at the drive-in."

"I'd love to," she said. "But Michael will be home and I should spend some time with him."

"Right. We'll do something else. The three of us. It'll give me a chance to know him. See you then. Unless..."

"Unless the Judson goat needs you."

"Or..."

"Understood."

STILL FEELING A GLOW the next morning, she sat at the kitchen table, staring at the coffeepot. She was trying to decide whether she wanted coffee badly enough to get up and actually make some. Outside were sounds of activity—the voices of Ed Collins and another man, the answering whinny of a horse.

She was too deep in her own thoughts to hear the car drive up. But she heard its door slam. She heard the scritching of the gate and the thumping of feet on the front porch.

"Hi, honey," she said brightly as her brother appeared.

Scowling, he only looked at her but didn't answer as he flew past to find the back room that was now his. The door closed with a bang.

"Michael?"

"Leave him alone," Leigh advised, collapsing into one of the battered kitchen chairs. "He needs to cool off."

"What happened? Not a fight, I hope."

"It came *that* close." She measured the distance of half an inch between her thumb and forefinger. "Some kids at the service station were teasing him, I forget what about. He lost his temper. Wow. He's got a mouth on him, that brother of yours."

"Oh, Leigh, I'm sorry."

"Don't sweat it." She grinned crookedly. "He nearly took a swing at me when I made him get into the truck. He wanted to stand his ground against the three of them."

"I'd better have a talk with him."

"No. It's me he'd like to clobber. Besides, his blowups don't last long. He just needs to think things over."

"His blowups—plural?" Tracy groaned. "You mean..."

"There was a slight tussle last night. One of the kids criticized the way he sat his saddle."

"Super."

"Why don't you fix us some coffee and let me handle our pint-sized Rocky?"

"You're so patient with him."

"Why not? I love kids. Maybe I'll have some of my own before long. If I can't have them, we'll adopt."

"We? You and this special Mr. Somebody? Uh-oh. This sounds serious."

"It is."

"Then *you* sit down. I'll reheat the coffee and we'll talk about it. You said I used to know him. Who is he?"

"You'll never guess."

"I don't want to guess. Just tell me."

"I don't know where to start. He's handsome, tall and virile."

Tracy set the coffeepot on the stove. "Mmm. That's a good start."

"He has a terrific sense of humor and he's great with kids. Sound familiar?"

"Not yet."

"Okay—how about this, then? He's an expert on anything to do with Indians. He's part Indian himself. One-quarter Blackfoot, to be exact."

Tracy switched the flame on too high under the coffeepot and nearly burned her hand. "He's part Indian? Blackfoot?"

"What's wrong with that?" Leigh was instantly defensive.

"Nothing. Nothing's wrong with that." Tracy said abruptly. "What's his name?"

"I might as well tell you." Leigh's voice was still sullen. "It doesn't matter, anyway. You went out with him for a while. Actually, he was one of your rejects." Then, more cheerfully, "Why do I have this intense craving for peanut butter and honey on whole-wheat bread? I guess it's love."

"Who is he?" Somehow Tracy managed to keep a calm exterior to belie the fact that she was quivering inside. Please don't let it be Ryle. Please.

"I don't really blame you for unloading him, though."
Leigh opened the cabinet to get the makings for her sandwich. "He was all arms and legs. His feet were like boats
and he was always stumbling over things because he had his
nose in a book."

"He...he sounds like a real winner."

"That's why I knew you'd never guess who he is." Leigh's
laugh was musical. She spread one slice of bread with honey
and the other with peanut butter before licking her knife and
putting the two slices together. "He doesn't look like that
anymore. You've heard of the Ugly Duckling? He's filled
out—and I do mean filled out. He has the most fantastic
build, know what I mean? His eyes are gorgeous, soft and
dark brown like Bambi, but they can bore right into you.
Mmm, what else? His hair is dark blond with sensational
sun streaks through it. Guessed yet? Okay, one last clue: he's
a vet. Oh, come on! It's Ryle Tanner! You remember Ryle
Tanner, don't you?"

CHAPTER FOUR

LEIGH'S WORDS seemed to echo through the room. You remember Ryle Tanner, don't you? Ryle Tanner. Ryle Tanner.

Tracy swallowed. "Have you been dating long?"

"We haven't dated at all in the usual sense of the word. Not yet, anyway."

"Then how can you be so sure of what you feel about him?"

"I'm sure." There was a pause. "Uh, Trace, for now it's confidential, okay? Promise me you won't say anything."

Tracy shook her head impatiently. "No...no, I won't say anything. But Leigh, how can you possibly know what he feels about you?"

"He's a busy guy, Trace. Too busy for your mundane movie-and-popcorn kind of relationship. He's serious. Not stodgy, mind you. But serious. He comes into the kitchen though, every time he's here to see one of the horses. Naturally I call him if one of them even looks as if it might sneeze. Then I fix him one of my special sandwiches. He loves to eat. And we talk on and on. I can tell by the way he looks at me that he cares. He enjoys our quiet times together. Sometimes I bring him out of himself and make him laugh. He's so cute when he laughs. But he's kind of shy with women. It's going to take real psychology on my part to make him declare himself."

Tell her now, Tracy warned herself. You have to tell her before it's too late. That you and Ryle are seeing each other again. That things are special between you. You're sorry, but it can't be helped. Tell her.

"Needless to say, my girl, hands off," Leigh went on. "If you want to keep that beautiful head of hair, that is. This is not just another man. This is what they mean when they say 'once in a lifetime.' So, you may speak to him about the weather, should you find yourself in the same room with him and talk seems called for. But keep your eyes on the floor. After the engagement, I'll allow you to take a good look at him. No. On second thought, make that after the wedding."

"How can you be sure it's the real thing when you've never even talked to him about it? How can you possibly know what he—"

"I can't explain, Trace," Leigh broke in, clasping her hands together and bringing them to her mouth. "It's a feeling that...that's just there. It doesn't need any words. You'll understand someday when it happens to you."

Someday when it happens to you. Someday. And now Tracy knew that her "someday" would have to be with someone else. She owed Leigh this chance to build a relationship with Ryle; perhaps, in time, he would feel for Leigh what she felt for him.

Leigh deserved to find happiness. But why did she have to go and fall in love with Ryle? *Why Ryle?* And now Tracy couldn't tell her the truth, couldn't stand in her way. Not after the years of friendship. Not after everything Leigh had done for her. Even getting her the shop—giving her a second chance.

She suddenly realized that Leigh was looking at her curiously. "Tracy! Hey, Trace. Wake up! Isn't it time you got dressed?"

"Dressed for what?"

"You have to register Michael at school this morning, don't you?"

Tracy squeezed her eyes shut. "Maybe I won't. There are only a couple of weeks left of the school term anyway."

"Don't fall into that trap, my girl." Leigh caught a drip of honey with her tongue before starting in on her sandwich. "Michael needs these last days to make friends. Otherwise it'll be that much harder for him to get acquainted with anyone through the summer. He'll be bored silly, out of sorts and under foot."

"He won't like it." Tracy was in no mood to hold her ground against the obstinate nine-year-old.

"He's already agreed. We talked about it on the way to Moberly."

"I wish I knew your secret."

"I'll never tell. Do you want a sandwich?"

"No thanks. I'd better get dressed."

"Pour yourself a coffee first. You look as though you could use it. I'll have a whack at Michael. Maybe he'll shake hands over peanut butter and honey."

Tracy's head began to throb. The phone book. Where was the phone book? She had to call Ryle and cancel their date. At least until she'd had a chance to think. What excuse could she give him? He obviously had no idea how Leigh felt about him. And she couldn't tell him. She couldn't betray Leigh's confidence. She'd just have to invent something, anything, even if it sounded ridiculous.

Should she try him at home or at the office? It was early yet. Home, she decided. Where was that book?

Too late. Leigh was back with Michael in tow. While he wasn't grinning, his face wouldn't have turned anyone to stone, either. "I'd rather have jelly than honey with my peanut butter," he said.

"We have a gourmet here. Raspberry or grape?"

"Grape. Raspberry has those dumb seeds that get stuck between my teeth." Michael heaved himself onto the chair beside Tracy. "Are you having one, Trace?"

"Your sister's not the peanut butter type," Leigh told him. "She doesn't know what she's missing."

Tracy smiled woodenly, not knowing what she was smiling about. All she could think of was Ryle and how she could get to him before it was too late.

MICHAEL'S ENROLLMENT went smoothly, though it took agonizingly long, with Tracy keeping one eye on the clock. There were papers to be signed and emergency forms, as well as records of inoculations. Mrs. Campbell, who would be his teacher, was young, attractive and conscientious. She wanted a detailed explanation of some of the comments on Michael's last progress report. Tracy told her about his oversensitivity to criticism and about the many uprootings he'd already experienced and his inability to get along with his stepfather. The woman took notes as she listened, alternately smiling and frowning.

The structured program at Edison Elementary School would be exactly what the boy needed, Mrs. Campbell thought. Sister and teacher would have to keep in close contact though, just to be sure.

It was after nine-thirty before Tracy could escape. What if Ryle had already called the stables and talked to Leigh? "Tell Tracy I have to cancel our date for tonight," he'd say. "Something came up."

Our date for tonight.

Maybe not. Maybe he'd be too busy to call. Maybe.

She *had* to get to him before he could say anything to Leigh. Preoccupied, Tracy climbed into the car and headed straight for his office. But less than a mile from the center of town, smoke began pouring from the Plymouth's hood. The car hadn't been getting enough attention to suit it lately. By the time she called a service station and had it towed, another hour was lost. The radiator hose had broken. She hardly heard the mechanic as he discussed the Plymouth's other ailments and what should be done about them. What if Ryle stopped by the stables on his way to see a patient?

"I just wanted to say hi," he'd tell Leigh. "And tell Tracy how much I enjoyed last night."

Why hadn't she been honest with her friend? "I didn't know Ryle was the one you cared about," she could have said. "I'm sorry, but we've picked up where we left off more than ten years ago. We've always cared about each other and didn't realize it until now."

No, she couldn't have done that. Poor Leigh had always been unlucky in love, from the time she had a crush on a crew-cut terror in the third grade until the last and most devastating episode, when she'd fallen in love with that lawyer. After his deception, Leigh seemed to lose her self-confidence completely. Tracy remembered her sobbing uncontrollably on the phone. She remembered the anguish and self-ridicule that had seeped from between the lines of her friend's letters.

But eventually the old Leigh had emerged, a little less trusting, a little less hopeful. Until she'd started having these romantic ideas about Ryle. And even though Tracy was convinced the ideas were all Leigh's, she couldn't interfere. Leigh's emotional stability was still shaky, and telling her about Ryle now would be cruel. Doubly cruel. Not only the humiliation of another rejection but the agony of betrayal—by her best friend. No, it was impossible.

"Tracy? Tracy Whelan?" A voice from the past jerked her back to the service station again and to the man droning on about her aging car.

But it wasn't the mechanic who had called her. If she'd wanted to search the pathways of her entire life and choose the one person she never wanted to see again, it would have been Howard Barclay, hands down. Scott's father. The man walking toward her now.

He must have been about fifty, but he didn't look it. He was still perversely attractive with his strong features and his lean build. And he still had the same authoritative bearing. The biggest change in his appearance was his hair, now more gray than black.

"Trouble with your car?" he asked.

"No," she snapped. "I have it towed every now and then just to give it a rest."

He ignored that. "I heard you were back in town. Can I offer you a lift somewhere?"

To the state line, perhaps? "One of the advantages of small-town living is that everything is within walking distance."

"My car is across the street."

"No, thank you."

The prospect of casual conversation with Howard Barclay was ludicrous. The last time they'd seen each other was at the police station. He'd cursed her and threatened her with everything short of life-imprisonment. He'd sounded off to all who would listen about how she'd destroyed his innocent son's reputation and his life. She couldn't pretend they were old friends. But continuing a bitter feud didn't make much sense, either.

"Maybe you could tell me the quickest way to get to the veterinarian's office. Dr. Ryle Tanner?"

"I'll walk you there. It isn't far."

"No need."

"I'm going that way anyhow." He smiled and touched two fingers to his forehead as an elderly woman passed and spoke his name. "You took over the beauty parlor, I heard. The woman who had it before was slovenly. It'll be a lot of work getting it in shape."

"I'm not afraid of work."

"I'd like to help you, if you'd let me. To make up for the past."

Was he actually admitting he'd been wrong? It didn't seem possible. "Help me, how?"

"Any way I can. I realized too late how much Scotty depended on your friendship. If you had still been here when he came out of that place, maybe he would have..." He broke off and cleared his throat. "There isn't much good in going over what's done, is there?"

"No, there isn't."

"My wife and I are no longer together. And my father died not long after Scotty—Scotty's accident."

Tracy spotted the Pet Clinic sign and began to walk faster. "I'm sorry, Mr. Barclay."

"Call me Howard. Please. Would it be possible to have lunch together sometime? To talk things over?"

The child within her almost shot back a furious refusal, complete with devastating accusations. Instead, she managed to say quietly, "I don't see much point in it."

"Scott still talked about you at the last. I don't think he ever forgave himself for what he did to you. Or me for treating you as I did. But he was my only son. I couldn't believe he was capable of...of..."

"I know." She realized she sounded abrupt. But Howard Barclay had appeared too suddenly. She just wasn't prepared to mouth the reassuring platitudes that might have eased his discomfort. "I'm sorry, but I'm in a dreadful rush," she said. "Goodbye, Mr. Barclay."

She heard him say he'd wait for her to come back out as she pushed open the door and hurried into Ryle's office, conscious of Howard's eyes still on her.

"Hi!" The girl who sat in the waiting room was about nineteen or twenty. She had very short, curly black hair and huge blue eyes. She offered Tracy a firm hand. "Welcome back."

"Should I know you?"

"Not really. I was a mere babe when I saw you last. I'm Suzanne. Scotty's baby sister."

"Oh, yes." This was her day for Barclays, it seemed. She'd known Scott had a sister but she'd hardly ever seen her. Tracy wasn't allowed within a stone's throw of the Barclay estate in those days.

"I saw you and Daddy talking and ducked in here to hide. I'm supposed to be working." The girl eyed her critically. "Do you know Doc Tanner?"

"We went to school together."

"Is this a personal visit, or are you picking up an animal?"

Tracy didn't have time to answer. At that moment Ryle emerged from one of the inner rooms and saw her. He wore a green coverall style apron and a curious smile. "What's up? If you'd come a minute later, you'd have missed me. I'm on my way out."

"I won't keep you."

"Don't mind me, Ryle," Suzanne chirped. "I'm hiding from Daddy again."

"Wouldn't it be easier just to stay on the job?"

"On a heavenly day like this?"

Tracy walked down the hallway and into the room Ryle had just left. She didn't want the girl to overhear their conversation. "I came to tell you I've changed my mind about our going out tonight," she said when he'd followed her.

"No problem. I've got a lot of correspondence to catch up on anyway. The lady who does part-time office work for me and Doc Cole will be in tomorrow, so I should get my stuff ready for her to type." As he spoke he took off his apron and hung it in the closet, then turned back to her, rolling up his sleeves. The face of his watch was very large with black numbers, and the time was incorrect by several hours.

"Your watch has stopped," she said. She couldn't keep the surprise out of her voice.

"I didn't set it this morning. Guess I had other things on my mind." His eyes grazed her lips, warning that she was about to be kissed unless she acted quickly. "Shall we get together tomorrow night instead?" he asked.

This was going to be considerably more difficult than she'd expected. Even here in the clinical atmosphere of the examining room, with its medicine cabinets and stainless steel tables, she wanted to touch him. And she wanted him to touch her.

"What about Michael?" She paused. "And Leigh?" She watched his face carefully.

"Bring them along."

"You wouldn't mind Leigh coming, too?"

"Why should I? She's a good friend."

It hadn't really been necessary to check his reaction to Leigh's name. Tracy should have known that the passing years hadn't changed Ryle's basic nature. He'd never encouraged Leigh. And he clearly had no idea how she felt about him.

"Well, actually, tomorrow night isn't good, either," she managed.

"Oh?" One of his eyes narrowed. He'd sensed that all wasn't well.

"I don't think it's wise for us to see each other anymore."

"Have I been rushing you?" His voice was studiedly calm.

"No. You've been very nice."

"Then . . ."

"I've decided I shouldn't get involved with any of the old crowd."

He smoothed a hand across the surface of the table. "Since when was I part of the crowd?"

"You know what I mean."

"No. Tell me."

"You represent yesterday. An ugly, painful yesterday I have to put behind me if I'm going to make my life here work."

"Isn't Leigh part of the old crowd?"

"Not really. Besides, she and I have never been out of touch. She's my best friend. Anyway, you know what I mean. *Romantically* involved."

"You didn't seem too worried about getting involved last night."

"I know. Last night was a mistake."

"Oh, is that what it was?"

"Yes, I'm sorry if I've hurt you, but it can't be helped. I'd better go now."

He caught her arm, not gently, as she turned to leave. "I can't believe last night didn't mean anything to you."

"It was very nice. But last night was last night. I don't intend to... relive the past."

"Relive the past?" His fingers dug into the flesh of her upper arm as he jerked her toward him. Color streaked his face. "I thought that's exactly what you did want."

"You were wrong."

"I don't think so."

The phone rang, but he didn't release her or make a move toward it. He only stared at her, boring into her eyes with his.

"This discussion is pointless." Tracy winced, more from the searing heat of his anger than from pain. "You're hurting me."

He released her arm immediately, but his eyes still held hers.

"Ryle." Suzanne stood in the doorway, wearing a quizzical little half smile. "Mrs. Boyle is on the line. I took the liberty of answering."

"Ask her to hold."

"Take your call," Tracy told him. "I'm leaving."

"You'll leave when this...discussion is finished," he said through clenched teeth, not deterred by the fact that they had an audience. "I sure as hell deserve a better explanation than the one you've given me."

"It's the only one you're going to get."

"Hey, you two," Suzanne chided. "What's going on?"

Ryle didn't seem to notice her. "Dammit, Tracy," he said harshly. "What we shared last night wasn't a lie."

He pulled her toward him and caught her around the waist. His breath was warm against her mouth and she felt as if she were sinking. If he kissed her, she would be lost.

With all her strength, she pressed her fingers against his chest and leaned back to avoid his lips. "Wasn't it? Like most men, you believe what you want to believe. Anything that satisfies your ego."

The iciness in her voice caught him off guard and he re-laxed his hold. She broke free and squeezed past Suzanne. The girl had to press herself against the wall to keep from getting caught between them as Ryle sprang after her.

"This isn't finished," he yelled.

"As far as I'm concerned, it is."

"Yikes!" Suzanne tugged at Ryle's arm and pointed to-ward the front office. "Daddy's coming. If he sees me, I'm cooked."

"Your father?" Ryle's curse was colorful and explicit. "What the hell does he want?"

"I think he's here for Tracy. They arrived together, too. May I hide in the other room until they're gone?"

"Tracy?" Clearly Ryle was stunned.

The door opened and Howard Barclay looked in just as Suzanne disappeared into the small examining room. "Are you finished yet?" he asked Tracy.

"Yes, Howard, I am. Thank you for waiting." She flashed him her most dazzling smile. Suzanne's oddly coy remark had given Tracy an idea; she suddenly saw in How-ard a chance to discourage Ryle completely.

"Doctor," Howard said, nodding at Ryle as he offered Tracy his arm.

Ryle snatched up the phone and turned away, but not be-fore she saw the look of sheer fury on his face. "Mrs. Boyle," he said in a constricted voice. "What can I do for you?"

"I was sure you'd change your mind when you thought about it," Howard said when they were outside. "It's a long walk, if you're headed back to Leigh Monahan's place."

"I don't mind walking," she retorted, too dead inside to care that he'd waited for her despite her wishes.

"Listen, Tracy, I don't want to bother you, but I had to try again. My offer of assistance is genuine—no strings at-tached. Please believe that. And please accept it—for Scotty's sake."

"I'm grateful, Mr. Barclay. But I don't need any help. So far, I'm doing fine."

He opened the door of his large luxurious car and ushered her in. "You might find it necessary to take out a bank loan, or get credit with some of the stores, here or in Moberly. Whatever your opinion of me personally, I think you'll agree that the Barclay name carries a lot of weight in this area. It impresses people, makes them more inclined to be cooperative."

Tracy just couldn't let that pass. "It's your grandfather who impresses them," she reminded him sharply. "Or whoever it was who made your family's fortune to begin with."

He threw his head back and laughed. "My great-great-grandfather, Wilson Barclay. He made his money by heroically trampling on everyone who got in his way. The rest of us only stumble along in his footsteps."

Tracy stared at him. He was mocking his own wealth and prestige—something the Howard Barclay of ten years before would never have done. Perhaps the man really had changed. He'd suffered, losing most of his family to death or divorce. And suffering changed people. His daughter was all he had left. A daughter who ran into other people's offices to hide from her father. Tracy couldn't help wondering about the problems between them. Was Howard too hard on Suzanne? Or was Suzanne just a spoiled brat? What kind of game had she been playing back there in Ryle's office, anyway? Tracy cringed, imagining Ryle's thoughts now. Maybe he'd think she was making up to Mr. Barclay because of his money. Maybe he'd even think Howard was the reason she'd canceled their date. Well, wasn't that what she wanted him to think?

"My life started to fall apart after my son died," Howard said.

"I'm sorry," she murmured, looking at him in surprise that he had reflected her thoughts.

"Scotty marched to a different drummer, as they say. But I didn't realize it then. You were the only one who understood."

It was odd, she thought, as they rode toward the stables in silence. She'd been so in awe of Howard Barclay once. Now she pitied him.

When he reached over to let her out, he closed a hand over hers briefly. "Let me make up for the hurt I caused you. Please."

"It was a long time ago."

"We had to blame someone, his mother and I. It's no excuse, but you were unfortunate enough to be handy."

In a sense, her hatred for him all those years had comforted her, given her reason to fight. Now, without that hatred, she felt as if she were drifting. Last night she'd found an anchor in the beauty and wonder of Ryle's feelings for her, feelings that could easily have grown into deep and lasting love. Now those feelings were gone, too.

And there was no help for it.

CHAPTER FIVE

Two WOMEN stopped to watch the sign painter as he put the finishing touches on his handiwork. Tracy's Hair Design, it now proclaimed in swirling gold letters that glittered in the sun. The name was one she'd tucked in the back of her mind years before, when she'd first begun to think about opening her own salon. The pink-and-gold metallic paper in the waiting area was another long-planned idea.

She'd explained her decorating theories to Leigh and Michael the night before. "It might be cheaper just to slather everything with white—like Tom Sawyer's fence," she'd said, "but that's not the atmosphere I want. I'm going after a total image. You know, feminine. Soft-sell glamour."

When Leigh had hesitantly referred to the cost of replacing the floor tile and using such extravagant wallpaper, Tracy had objected. "How could anyone feel glamorous staring at clinical white walls and that odious floor? No, I've thought this out very carefully. I'm just going to have to cut back somewhere else."

Ever since that disastrous visit to Ryle's office Tracy had thrown herself into remodeling the salon. She poured all her energy, all her waking thoughts into the work, as much to forestall brooding about Ryle as to get the shop ready for business.

The thought of Ryle still hurt terribly and the yearning for him disturbed her sleep more nights than it didn't. But that would pass with time, wouldn't it?

Now and then she caught sight of him on the street, but so far only at a distance, and there was enough warning so that she could take another route and avoid coming face-to-face with him.

Another person she tried to avoid was Suzanne Barclay, who had started dropping in unannounced. She'd bring Tracy a coffee or a magazine and stay to chat—about the shop or the town, but mostly about herself. Tracy would half listen, intent on her own work. Just what Suzanne wanted from her was something she hadn't yet figured out.

Suzanne would sprawl on one of the old salon chairs, talking a mile a minute. She'd complain about her "trivial" job on the town newspaper, a job her father had arranged for her. She often talked about her father, in fact, bitterly reviling what she called his unfairness to her. Occasionally, though, she'd speak of him with warmth and even affection.

Tracy sensed a brittleness in Suzanne that she distrusted. The girl's comments were sarcastic and sometimes amusing, but too often merely vicious. Tracy responded noncommittally if at all, trying to discourage Suzanne's confidences and overtures of friendship—if friendship was indeed what Suzanne was after.

Leigh had a few things to say on the matter. "She's using you, Trace. I don't know why. But she wants something." And when Tracy suggested that perhaps Suzanne just needed a friend, Leigh snorted in disgust. "Hah! That bitch—oops, sorry to insult your species, Willie-boy—that creature doesn't know the meaning of the word friend."

Tracy just sighed. Leigh disliked Suzanne so intensely that she hardly ever visited the shop anymore for fear of running into her. It was just as well. When the two got together the conversation turned into a verbal sparring match, with Suzanne, who remained surprisingly coolheaded, invariably getting the best of it.

"She's a Barclay, isn't she?" Leigh would ask whenever Tracy tried to smooth things over between them. "Since when are you so charitable toward that family?"

Tracy looked up from the bills she was paying to see the two women—potential clients?—still standing outside. She smiled at them and decided that now was as good a time as any to do a public relations job. She vaguely remembered the women's faces, but not their names.

She got up and went to the door. "Hello, I'm Tracy Whelan," she said brightly as she stepped outside.

"Taking over Irma's old place, are you?" The woman thrust a finger under her scarf to adjust one of the pin curls it covered.

"Yes. I plan to open in a week or so."

"I don't know that you'll do much business." The other woman, shorter and stouter than her friend, smoothed a pleat in her dress sleeve. "This place has been closed so long. Irma went to live with her daughter. Folks got used to driving to Moberly when the other shop on Chestnut was booked."

"Now they won't have to do that." Tracy gave them another smile for good measure.

"I don't know. We're plain folks here. Not many of us want movie-star hairdos." She frowned and looked over her glasses at the pictures of attractive models Tracy displayed in the window.

"Too bad Irma had to go," the woman with pin curls said. "She knew what we wanted."

Turner. Wasn't her name Turner? Constance—Clara—something Turner. "I'm certain I'll be able to please you, too, if you'll give me the opportunity." She handed each of them one of the pink-and-gold cards she'd picked up at the printer's that morning. It would entitle them to twenty percent off on their first visit.

The stout woman handed the card back and folded her hands across her ample stomach. "Now, it's not that I mind paying the price. It's just that I know what I want. Besides, the shopping is better in Moberly. They have a cafeteria there, too."

The other woman nodded in agreement, and they moved off down the street.

"Have a nice day," Tracy called after them.

"You're gonna find a lot of that around here," the sign painter said in an irritating monotone. "New businesses are hard to start up. Most of 'em fail."

Tracy ignored his comment. "Would you like a discount card for your wife? She can save twenty percent on getting her hair done."

He hooted. "She can save one hundred percent by fixing her own hair like she's been doing the thirty-one years we've been married."

Tracy turned away, determined that his pronouncement wouldn't dash her joy in the glittering new window. Actually things had gone far better than she'd expected. The shop looked wonderful and doing most of the work herself meant that her costs had been lower than she'd anticipated. She'd be able to survive for three months longer without profit than she'd originally calculated.

When she had paid the sign painter and he'd gone, she decided to exercise one of the rights of self-employment, and leave for the day. She'd drive home, have lunch and take Roxy, Leigh's temperamental little mare, out on the trail again. All those years in the city hadn't made her lose her love of horses and riding. All her ramblings in the hills since she'd come back hadn't made the scenery seem familiar or boring. The sky was ever-changing. The colors of nature were always new. Bird songs were beloved and welcome melodies, far more soothing than any music she could have tuned in on the radio.

When her brother came home, she decided as she sped along the road to the stables, they'd drive around and distribute the discount cards.

Maybe he could even invite his new friend to come with them. To Tracy's profound relief, Michael was doing well in school; he'd only been in trouble once. And he'd actually made a friend. The boy, Dave, was the passive type her brother usually chose, someone he could order around. But he was a friend, all the same. Michael had joined the youth group at Leigh's prodding, had completed a simple woodworking project and would be going on the camp-out with Ryle in another week.

Ryle. There he was, creeping into her thoughts again. She tightened her lips in pain and forced herself to think about distributing the discount cards. She'd have to map out a route and then she and Michael and maybe his friend could each take a few streets. The cards were an inspired idea—Leigh's idea, really. No wait, Leigh had mumbled something about Ed Collins suggesting it. Tracy sighed wearily—yet another person she couldn't figure out. Anyway, the plan was a good one. Surely some of the town's inhabitants would be pleased not to have to take the jaunt to Moberly when they wanted their hair done. Surely out of five hundred cards she'd get fifty takers.

As she concentrated on negotiating the rough driveway with its deep muddy furrows, she was suddenly jolted by the sight of Ryle's station wagon in front of the house.

"Now what?" she groaned aloud. She slowed, looked over her shoulder and prepared to turn around and go back. But Leigh was on the porch and had already spotted her. She'd been crying. Her eyes were swollen and watery.

"The new pony's sick," she wailed when Tracy got out of the car. "Can you go in and help Ryle? Ed's in there now, but he's probably just getting in the way." She sniffed back her tears. "He's even more of a baby than I am when it comes to the animals. And I've got to leave now. I have to give a private riding lesson."

"Let me give the lesson for you. I know how. Remember? Then you can go in and help."

"No." Leigh began to wring her hands. "My students are a little girl and her littler brother. They're both shy of strangers. Besides, I couldn't stand to watch. Ryle's going to have to stick some horrible long tube down my pony's throat."

Tracy reluctantly entered the stable to find the pony lying on the floor of her stall, making blowing noises. Ryle was bent over her, sleeves rolled up, the back of his shirt drenched with perspiration. Ed Collins knelt beside him, his face pale and drawn.

"What can I do to help?" Tracy offered, forgetting her own worries at the sight of the animal in obvious pain. "You can help by getting out of here," Ryle told her coldly.

Damn him. She could have kicked Ryle for talking to her as if she were a pesky child, especially in front of Ed Collins. Though Ed hardly seemed to notice she was there.

The two men were having a time getting the pony to her feet. Sick as she was, she was putting up a gallant fight. Ryle would have to tranquilize her, he said, before he could do anything.

"Is it serious?" Tracy asked, moving out of their way as they struggled.

"Are you still here?" Ryle shot back. "Make some coffee if you want to do something useful."

Right away, boss. Yessir, boss, she grumbled to herself as she stormed into the house. Good old Doc Tanner was sorely lacking in stall-side manners. Or maybe it was reserved for the animals.

"Make some coffee," she repeated. There was still some on the stove from breakfast. Reheated coffee would be good enough for Mr. Charming.

The leftover potato salad in the refrigerator reminded her that she hadn't eaten anything since breakfast. She scooped some onto her plate, along with two slices of salami, and settled in the breakfast nook with a tall glass of iced tea and a back issue of *Glamour* magazine. As if she'd be able to eat much, or even read, with Ryle just outside.

It was a brave attempt, but she gave up. After a soothing shower, she combed her hair, working over it until it curled obediently in all the right places. Her sleeveless green-and-white candy-striped blouse and green cotton skirt seemed to be an appropriate outfit. It would be cool, but still businesslike enough for the delivery of the cards. In another forty minutes or so, Michael would be home and they could begin their rounds.

"Where's that coffee, Whelan?" She started at the sound of Ryle's voice. He'd come in without knocking. The bluish circles under his eyes made him look as if he'd been the loser in a barroom brawl. He obviously hadn't got much sleep and his shadowy jawline said he hadn't shaved either.

Tracy softened at the sight of him. "The coffee in the pot is from this morning. I'll make some fresh. I didn't know how long you'd be."

"Forget it. I don't care if it's strong enough to pour itself into the cup. It'll do."

"How's the pony?"

"Ed's walking her. It was indigestion."

"That's all?"

"Indigestion can be serious in a horse, and damned painful." He sat at the table, planted his elbows on it and pressed his fingers against his eyes. "She'll be okay."

"Good." Tracy took a coffee mug from its hook, looked at it and replaced it for another without a chip. She set a saucer under it and poured the strong-smelling brew. Quickly she moved away, hoping he couldn't see that her hands were trembling.

"How's the shop coming?"

"The signs are up. And I'm slowly but surely getting the news out to people. There'll be an ad in the paper starting Monday." She told him about her pink-and-gold color scheme, about how nice the wallpaper looked and about the cards she'd had printed. She knew she was jabbering but it didn't matter. She couldn't stop.

He gave her a smoldering look that cut through her chatter and immediately silenced her. "Sit down. You make me nervous."

"I have to tell Leigh about the pony. She's worried sick."

"She's on the trail."

"I'll ride out to her."

He snorted. "In that skirt?"

She laughed at herself and shrugged. "I can ride side-saddle."

He peered over the top of his cup. "I think you're afraid to be alone with me."

"Should I be?"

"Not today, lady." He raised both hands in a gesture of surrender. "I promise not to lay a hand on you. To tell you the truth, I haven't got it in me. I'm beat."

"I wasn't thinking anything like that."

"Weren't you? I apologize for our last meeting. I usually manage to control my temper."

"Neither of us behaved very well."

"I could have handled it better. You were always an unpredictable little screwball. But I finally thought I had you figured out. You knocked me on my keester with that garbage about wanting to escape the past and me along with it."

"I meant what I said."

"Pardon me if I don't believe you. I haven't got your problem figured out yet—but I will. I need a little time. Maybe you think people will see us together and it might hurt my practice. You still have this overblown idea of the people in this town holding grudges. Is that it? It's nonsense, you know."

"That isn't it." She sighed. How could she let him know that nothing could happen between them—ever—without telling him about Leigh? And if she were to tell him about Leigh, she'd be revealing things her friend had told her in confidence. Leigh would never forgive her.

"Your heart was in your kisses, Tracy," he said. "Your heart and your soul. I'd stake my life on it."

"You'd lose. We were school chums. We hadn't seen each other in a long time. I was deeply moved."

"You hadn't seen Howard Barclay in a long time, either. Did he get the same treatment?" His right eye narrowed. His outrage was still there, seething under the surface. She knew it. And *he* knew that she knew it. "I think not. Look, the fires and that whole mess—it was a long time ago. People have forgotten, no matter what they might have believed back then. Now, nobody cares. So why don't you forget it, too?"

"Can I get you some more coffee?" she asked, putting a period on their conversation.

"Bleh!" He grimaced comically. "Is that how you plan to get rid of me? Poison?"

"You asked for it." She moved over to the sink. Wanting to appear busy, she began washing the few dishes that were soaking there, giving each cup and plate far more attention than it required.

Ryle scraped back his chair and came up behind her. Moisture formed on her forehead and on her upper lip. Her heart felt as if it had stopped. Did she have the strength to fight him again? Did she have enough strength to fight herself?

He lifted the hair at the back of her neck and blew, a small, cool flow of air. "You're soggy."

"It's humid," she said, steeling herself against him.

He brushed the hair away from her face and touched the tip of his tongue to her ear. She almost dropped the glass she was holding. "Stop that."

"Why should I?"

"For one thing, Leigh might come in."

His mouth moved to the side of her neck. "She's a big girl. She understands these things."

The thought of Leigh renewed her determination. She slid away from him, dried her hands on the dish towel and investigated the inside of the coffeepot. "Will you be coming to the barn dance Leigh's planning to hold when she reopens the stables?"

"Is that an invitation?"

"I've got too much to do, getting the shop ready. I don't have time for such frivolity."

"Make time. Going to community affairs is an excellent way to get to know people again and to let them know you. Good public relations, too!"

"I don't like square dancing."

"You used to love it."

"That was a long time ago. Besides, you never paid enough attention to me to notice what I liked." Perhaps if she could remember and relive how she'd felt then, when he'd never had enough time for her, she could get angry at him all over again. It might help, she thought desperately.

"I noticed."

"You never did anything about it."

"I'm ready to make up for it now."

"It's too late." She thrust a kitchen chair between them to slow down his advance. "Look, I'm tired and you must be, too. Why don't you go home and go to bed?"

"Will you come with me?" He shoved the chair aside and closed the distance between them in a single step. "You smell like peppermint candy."

"Spearmint. I—I had a Lifesaver. Leigh's potato salad is wonderful, but . . ." Her train of thought abruptly derailed as Ryle traced the side of her face with one finger. "But it's full of onions."

"I wouldn't have cared."

"I wasn't thinking of you."

"Weren't you? You not only smell like peppermint-candy, but in that shirt, you look like it, too. Good enough to eat."

"Can I get you some potato salad?" Her voice had the hollow sound of an actress playing to an empty theater. "There's plenty left."

"Potato salad." A corner of his mouth quivered and lifted in an enigmatic smile. "There's something I want more. Come here."

"Ryle, you promised," she reminded him.

"I lied." His sinewy arms snared her before she could twist away. His fingers knotted in her hair to keep her still. They were so close together that her struggle only ground her body against his, arousing him all the more. And arousing her no less.

He didn't kiss her at once, but waited, his eyes sweeping her face and coming to rest on her lips, causing the smoldering embers of her desire to burst into flame.

"This is how it was meant to be, Tracy," he said, the mere movement of his lips drugging her into silence. "God, I want to kiss you. But I haven't shaved. Your skin is so soft. Mine would be like sandpaper against it."

"It's good for the complexion," she said softly, not meaning to say it aloud.

"Kissing?"

"Friction. It . . . helps the circulation."

"Then I'm prepared to supply you with a lifetime of free beauty treatments," he said, brushing her lips gently with his, far too gently to still the aching. His fingers skimmed over her back, remembering her body without possessing it—knowing her need without satisfying it. Incredible power lay in the restrained kiss and in the marvelous lightness of his hands.

His tongue slid over her lips, circled them, then went between them, probing, searching, tantalizing her beyond all reason. Softly crushed against him, her tingling breasts knew the heat of his skin beneath his shirt. The blood in her veins was a raging torrent.

Her fingers felt their way along his arms and up toward his neck, drawing his face down to complete the kiss. He mustn't stop now. He mustn't. She was aware of the salty taste of his skin and the faint musky smell that surrounded him. His mouth fastened on hers with a fierce sweetness. His arms tightened, almost lifting her off the floor.

From somewhere far away she was vaguely conscious of a sharp sound. A knock. And then again. Her eyes flew open. Time and place zoomed into focus. Ryle's mouth dragged itself from hers.

Ed Collins stood at the door watching them through the screen with a strange expression on his face. "Pony's okay, doc. Do you want me to put her back?"

"Not yet." Ryle didn't seem any more flustered than he'd been when Suzanne had watched them do battle. He didn't even release his hold. "I'll be with you in a minute."

"Is it okay if I don't hold my breath?" Ed muttered, and Tracy was shaken by the cold disgust she heard in his voice.

"Now where were we?" Ryle turned back to her.

"Don't kiss me." Tracy pulled away. "Ed saw us."

"I don't give a damn. I'm not ashamed of my feelings for you. I'd kiss you on the expressway overpass. On the stage of the Municipal Auditorium. In Leigh Monahan's kitchen."

"Well, I do give a damn." She pressed her fingers to her lips, burning now from the scraping of Ryle's beard.

"Oh, I'm sorry, honey," he said, concern shading his eyes. "Did I hurt you?"

"No."

So it had happened. The passion that had flared up so easily couldn't be taken back. But it mustn't happen again.

Unshed tears stung her eyes as she looked at him. A picture from the past stole through her thoughts. She and Ryle. Teenagers again. Walking together. Holding hands. Stopping to smile into each other's eyes. To share a quick kiss.

Something brushed against her leg and she looked down. There was Willie, roused from his nap and wanting to be noticed, wagging his whole body along with his tail. Tracy, welcoming distraction in any form, stooped down to pet him.

"He's too fat," Ryle said.

"He's ten years old. What do you expect?"

"He's too fat for any age. Stop feeding him at the table."

"Oh, but he's so cute when he's begging. I can't deny him anything."

"Really?" Ryle twisted his mouth to one side. "Maybe I should try it."

From the sudden commotion outside, it was obvious that Leigh had returned. They heard her in the yard, squealing over the pony and talking excitedly with Ed. Then she was running toward the house, her hair looking orange in the sunlight. Her face was flushed and scattered with new freckles.

"Oh, thank you, Ryle. Thank you for making her well. Thank you, thank you. I know how bushed you must be. You were out on emergency calls all night. Then here."

"Forget it."

"Sack out in the bedroom. I wouldn't let anybody bother you." There was such a vibrant glow in her eyes as she looked at him, how could he not know how she felt? Tracy wondered.

"No, thanks," he said. "I promised to check back on last night's patient before going home."

"You'd better start taking it easy, buster," Leigh admonished. "You'll get sick and then what will the poor four-footed ones in Council Grove do?"

Tracy opened the refrigerator and took out the ice water. She wasn't thirsty, but she couldn't stand listening to any more of Leigh's awkward flirting. It was wretched feeling as if she had betrayed her dearest friend. She'd had her chance with Ryle years ago and she'd given him up. Now Leigh was in love with him. Tracy had no place in the picture.

"Hi, baby." Noticing Willie at her feet, Leigh bent over to tousle the dog's shaggy fur and to favor him with some of her baby talk.

"I guess I'll go." Ryle looked at Tracy over Leigh's head. "How about riding along and keeping me company? We could stop somewhere for lunch. Better yet, we'll have a picnic. I'll stretch out on the grass and you can listen to me snore."

"That sounds like a reasonable offer, Leigh," Tracy said, her heart thudding as she did her best to divert the invitation. "Why *don't* you go? I can manage here."

As Leigh straightened up, her expression was blank. Surprise had left her numb—but only for an instant. Joy transformed her features. "Oh, I'd love to. Thank you, Ryle. I'll have to shower and change though, if you can wait."

"Oh . . . sure." Ryle's stare was glassy. It took him a moment to realize what had happened. Leigh had, with Tracy's help, assumed he was inviting her. His mouth sagged.

"Oh, no." Leigh clapped a hand to the top of her head. "I forgot I have a lesson at four."

"I'll take it," Tracy offered quickly, before Ryle could wriggle off the hook. "I used to give lessons in the long ago. Remember?"

"Oh, Trace, would you?"

"Of course. Go."

Tracy didn't dare look at Ryle's face. "What's the idea?" he muttered when Leigh had flown into the other room to change. "Was that your idea of a joke?"

Tracy poured her ice water and put the bottle back in the refrigerator. "I don't know what you're talking about."

"You know damn well what I'm talking about. I can see it in your eyes. I remember that look."

"You seem to remember an awful lot."

"And you don't seem to remember anything."

"Maybe that's because there's nothing to remember."

"Trace, would you come in here a sec?" Leigh called. "I need your advice."

She was holding up two dresses. One was pink and white and ruffly. The other was baby blue and ruffly. Neither would have looked right on Leigh. Tracy winced.

"Which?"

"You're going to check on a sick animal, remember? You may be at the farm for quite a while. Then you're going on a picnic. Wear your blue print blouse with either your blue skirt or your blue pants."

"But I want to dazzle him."

"Dazzle him by being you."

Not convinced, Leigh went into the bathroom, but was back in seconds to give Tracy a bone-crushing hug. "You're the most perfect friend a person could have. My whole life has changed since you got here. Do you think Ryle will ask me out if I hint around? Maybe a movie? A new one opened at the Peppertree last Friday. I forget who's in it, but it's supposed to be dripping with romance. It might give him a few ideas."

"Why don't you take this one step at a time?"

"Maybe that's the way you'd do it." Leigh was breathless with excitement. "But naturally, you couldn't understand how I feel about landing someone like Ryle."

"Why naturally?"

"Boys used to fall all over you. You could always take your pick."

"Wouldn't you admit to exaggerating a wee bit?"

"Nope. Me, I've waited and hoped and hoped and waited and prayed in between. Never daring to believe that a great, big wonderful hunk of a man like Ryle would actually notice me. Now he has, and I'm scared stiff I might do something wrong and lose him."

"Get ready then, before he leaves without you. He said he was in a hurry."

"Yikes! You're right. I won't be long."

Tracy slid into her own room and changed to her jeans for the riding lesson. Peeking around the corner, she could see Ryle. He stood at the screen door, one hand propped against the wall overhead, the other jammed into his pocket. Even with his back turned, she knew how his face would look.

In time maybe he would fall in love with Leigh. She told herself that Leigh could be quite attractive with a different hairdo and some judiciously applied makeup—something Tracy could do for her. Leigh was understanding and intelligent, and she had a great sense of humor, a prerequisite for an enduring marriage. Maybe someday Ryle would recall the episode in the kitchen. They'd laugh about it together. He'd even thank Tracy for playing Cupid.

"Funny," he'd say, "how things turn out for the best."

By then, Tracy might be able to agree and mean it.

As his station wagon disappeared around the bend, Suzanne's white convertible screeched into the driveway. Tracy pressed her lips together and blew a long, weary sigh. She wasn't in the mood for Suzanne's unpredictable behavior. Throwing an arm over her eyes to shield them from the sun, she went outside when she saw that Michael was sitting in the front seat.

"Hi, Trace," he yelled, spilling out of the car.

"Hi, yourself. No books?"

"No homework."

"You never have homework."

The boy allowed himself to be hugged briefly before skittering away. "I'm in a hurry. My friend from school—Dave—his mom said I could eat over."

"Don't you think you should have asked me?"

"You weren't there. His mom's making homemade ice cream. Strawberry."

"I need you to help deliver my discount cards."

"I'll help tomorrow." He was on the porch in less than a dozen steps and into the house. "I gotta get my catcher's mitt."

Suzanne lifted the full skirt of her red sundress gingerly and stepped out of the car. Obviously she'd managed to avoid the work force again. Her outfit would have been glaringly out of place in any office.

"Where'd you find the monster?" Tracy asked.

"He flagged me down at the bottom of the hill."

"Thanks for delivering him."

"He's a kick." The girl waved away her thanks with an impatient flutter of one hand. "I passed Ryle. Was that actually Leigh with him?"

"Yes."

"Is there no end to his acts of charity?" Suzanne took off her oversize sunglasses and smirked.

"I have a riding lesson. What can I do for you?"

"It must be catching. You took Leigh's riding lesson so she could go out with your guy? Talk about philanthropy. But then, you knew it was safe—Leigh Monahan doesn't exactly figure as competition, does she?"

"Wait a minute. What makes you assume that Ryle is my guy, as you put it?"

"Have you forgotten I was witness to that love spat you two had in his office?"

"You misinterpreted what you saw."

"Saw and heard?"

"You can't possibly believe that he and I—"

"I'm not a child, Tracy. I can feel the heat of sexuality in the battle between a man and woman if it's there. And it was there." The girl adjusted one spaghetti strap and shook her head in mock pity. "Poor Leigh. Poor pathetic girl—she doesn't have a chance, does she? Looks like last week's laundry and *such* a loser with the men."

Tracy could hardly contain her fury. "That's enough, Suzanne," she said with as much cold authority as she could muster.

But Suzanne went on as though Tracy hadn't even spoken. "Here's poor old Leigh, who just can't seem to hold onto a man. And then there's her friend Tracy, who's practically fighting them off. Why, she's got Ryle, the old boyfriend, and my beloved daddy, the new boyfriend and—"

This time Tracy was determined to put a stop to the girl's vindictive stream of words. "Cut it out, Suzanne," she said sharply. "You know damn well your father's not interested in me! And I'm not interested in your nasty little—"

To Tracy's horror, Suzanne's face suddenly contorted. Her body shook. "You—you—who do you think you are?" she shrieked. "How dare you talk to me like that?" The change that came over her made Tracy notice, for the first time, how much she looked like Scott. He'd had the same unreasoning temper, the same low flashpoint.

Then Suzanne squeezed her eyes shut and stiffened, visibly making a tremendous effort to control herself. "Forget it." Her voice was tight and strange sounding. "I have to go." She whirled around, the red skirt billowing. Tracy watched, astonished, as Suzanne dashed toward her car without a further word or a backward glance.

AFTER THE RIDING LESSON, showered again and back in her skirt and blouse, Tracy began her appointed rounds with the discount cards. As she trudged from house to house, she exchanged friendly remarks with a few people and received indifferent stares from a few more. At one door, a woman yelled at her to complain about putting "junk" in her mailbox.

"Junk! Thanks a lot. That makes me feel just great," Tracy muttered through clenched teeth.

She heard several people discussing her, and that didn't make her feel any better. She heard a fat, bearded man in a ripped T-shirt loudly telling a much younger woman that Tracy had been Scott Barclay's girl. It took Tracy several seconds of study to recognize the bloated face and to place him as one of Scott's old friends—though she still couldn't think of his name.

"Remember I told you about those two?" he was saying. "Hellcats, the both of them, tearing up the roads and driving the cops crazy. Her and Scott—man, they were something. Almost burned the whole town to the ground."

So the legend lived on.

Why, she wondered grimly, couldn't Council Grove be like other small towns? Why didn't people grow up and move away?

CHAPTER SIX

As SHE SAT at the front desk in her shop going over records of expenditures, Tracy was surprised by the number of people who paused to look in the window. Some even smiled before moving on. Apparently the cards had activated interest. It might not be long before she had to recruit an assistant. She'd already collected the names of several who'd told her they might be willing to work for her once the business was under way.

She mulled over her latest idea—a shocking pink uniform to go with the decor. Pink was a good color for her. It emphasized her naturally creamy complexion and offered a becoming contrast to her glossy brown hair. Besides, what was more luxuriously feminine than pink?

Deep in thought as she sketched a possible design for the uniform, she felt a pair of eyes on her. Before she even saw the person's face, she knew who it was. Ryle. She looked down instantly. Too late. He was coming inside.

She swung around on the stool, gathered up her notebooks and shoved them into the drawer. "For a man who's as busy as you claim to be, you have a lot of time for socializing."

"This isn't a social visit." His jawline looked very square. "I wish it were."

"What would you call it?"

"Have you been out front this morning?"

"No."

"I thought not." He wiped the back of one hand across his forehead.

"I came in the back way. I always do. Is there a law against it?"

He took her arm. "There's something you'd better see."

"Will you stop?" She pulled out of his grasp. "I can walk under my own power."

"Then walk."

"What is it? A tidal wave? An earthquake?"

"You're getting warm. Outside," he insisted, holding the door open so that she could pass.

"I know. Little green men have landed in a flying saucer. What am I— Oh no!" Her knees buckled as he took her shoulders and faced her squarely toward the stucco front of the shop.

Someone had used cans of spray paint on it. *Pyromaniac*, it shouted in a bold black scrawl. Red and orange paint, like accusing fingers of flame, shot obscenely around both sides of the window, framing it.

Ryle's arms circled her, offering support. "Probably a bunch of kids."

"Those 'great' kids you were telling me about?"

"Try not to get hysterical."

"I'm not hysterical. I'm sick."

"It isn't the end of the world. And if the culprits are somewhere, watching, it'll only give them the charge they wanted out of their prank."

"You define this as a prank? What should I do? Laugh?"

"No. We'll cover it before any more people get a chance to see it."

"No wonder everyone's been staring in at me and smiling. They think it's funny. They're on the side of whoever did this."

"Steady, Whelan. Don't turn paranoid on me. I'll tear over to the hardware store and get some paint. You go to the sheriff's office and make a report."

"What good will a report do?"

"If the sheriff is watching the place, whoever did this will think twice before trying it again."

"Maybe the sheriff will think it's as funny as all my dear fellow townspeople thought it was."

"Go, Tracy. Forget all those maybes."

"Do you know how many coats of paint it will take to cover this . . . this . . ."

"I know we can't cover it today. But I'll get some advice from the paint man. We should be able to obliterate the message and apply a base to hold the color you want."

"We?"

He grinned crookedly. "Didn't you tell me you were thinking of changing the color anyway?"

"I did not."

"Maybe I read your mind. Go on, Tracy." He gave her a nudge with his elbow. "Move your tail. I smell rain in the air and we don't want to be caught in the middle of the job."

When she visited the sheriff's office, the response was every bit as disappointing as she'd privately expected. "I can tell the boys to keep an extra watch," he drawled, when she told him what had happened. "That's about all."

"Can't you—I don't know—investigate who might have done it?"

"Think I might find the perpetrators with paint still on their hands? Maybe even a trail of dribbled paint leading up to their door?" The sheriff looked over his shoulder at his deputy and chuckled. All the while, his hands were moving, trying to fit the pieces of a plastic puzzle into a square. "I sympathize with you, Miz Whelan. But this isn't *Hawaii Five-O*. We've got a nice, quiet town here—no need to keep any bloodhounds."

"Couldn't you at least check to see who bought the paint?"

A piece of the puzzle rattled to the floor and he leaned over to pick it up. "June is fix-up month by tradition. Lawn furniture. Toys, bicycles, fences. I can't very well arrest somebody for wanting to make things look shipshape, now can I?"

"But those particular colors. . . ."

"Partiality for certain colors doesn't constitute a crime. As I said, we'll keep alert in case they strike again. Can't do more than that. Sorry."

Ryle had opened and stirred the paint by the time she got back. His sleeves were rolled up and he'd begun to work. He'd spread a plastic drop cloth in front of the show window and weighted it with stones to protect the sidewalk. A splotch of white paint already decorated his muscular forearm.

She watched him. For a long moment she stood there, thinking how much she loved him. Her heart was filled to the brim by the sight of this man working so feverishly to help her put things right, wanting to protect her. She'd have fallen apart if he hadn't been there, helping her bear the crushing weight of this hideous act of vandalism.

Leigh had been wrong when she'd compared Ryle to the Ugly Duckling. If he had been clumsy with large hands and feet when Tracy knew him before, she hadn't noticed. He'd always been someone special. Someone to cry with when things went wrong, to laugh with when they were right. But she couldn't count on having him to lean on anymore. Her obligation to Leigh came between them. Episodes such as this one only made the prospect of separation more painful.

"How much was all this?" She picked up a ballpoint pen and waited.

"We'll settle later. Haven't you got some old clothes you can change into?"

"Will you please tell me what I owe you? I want to write out a check while I think of it." She hated the chill of her own voice. It sounded crisp and bitchy and made her feel like Bette Davis in one of her more hateful roles.

"If I didn't know better, I'd think I was being dismissed."

"You are." Unflinching, she looked at him. "I've never believed in two people on a one-person job. I can handle this alone. I've calmed down now."

"It'll go faster with the two of us."

"Don't you have an office to go to? Patients waiting?"

"Doc Cole is taking over this afternoon. It's my day off."

"Fine. Why don't you lie out in the sun or go fishing? May I have the brush?"

"Be my guest." He slapped the brush into her hand. "About the paint. I'll send you a bill."

"Ryle," she called after him, weakening at the sight of his loping retreat. "I'm grateful for your moral support."

He stopped at the door and turned to give her a hard stare. "Sure you are."

STIFF AND WEARY from the hours spent painting, Tracy walked slowly up the path to the house. All she wanted now was a quick sandwich in the kitchen and a nice long soak in the tub. With maybe a magazine for company. But as she approached the kitchen door, the pungent smell of tomato sauce drifted toward her—and she remembered Leigh's promise of a special meal that evening. She groaned.

Still glowing from her outing with Ryle the day before, Leigh had prepared a spaghetti dinner, complete with garlic bread and tossed salad, to celebrate. Tracy was in no mood for a huge dinner—or a celebration—but she couldn't disappoint her friend. She feigned enthusiasm as she watched Leigh bustling around the kitchen, putting dishes on the table, stirring the sauce and holding out spoonfuls for Michael's approval. All the while, she chattered to Tracy about the wonderful time she'd had with Ryle. About how smart he was, how gentle and how clever. How they'd stopped for a hot dog on the way home and she wished she could have slipped it into her handbag.

"But then I don't suppose you could fit a hot dog between the pages of a scrapbook, could you?"

"Maybe if you flattened it first," Michael said, giggling. "When are we gonna eat? I'm starving."

"Soon. Trace, I hope you don't mind, but I asked Ed to supper. We've been going over the bills together all afternoon and he looked so hungry." She paused. "Of course, he always looks hungry. I've been trying for years to fatten him up."

Tracy did mind, but how could she say so? Sitting across the table from a disapproving Ed Collins wouldn't do much for her digestion. He made her feel vaguely uncomfortable at the best of times, but ever since the afternoon he'd caught her and Ryle kissing, she could barely look him in the eye.

"There's a lot more to Ed than what you see on the surface," Leigh went on, making fancy rabbit ears out of the paper napkins. "He used to ride in rodeos. Won a lot of prizes, too. Then he hurt his knee and couldn't ride for a while. He was just drifting—passing through our fair town—when Dad met him and brought him home. And the rest you know. We put him on the payroll and he turned out to be a really good worker."

"Why did he stay on?"

"I don't really know. We kept expecting him to pull out when his leg healed. But he never did. I guess he got tired of the rodeo life."

"Does he ever talk about it?"

"Not much. The big surprise came when I thought I'd have to sell and he marched in and plunked a stack of money on the kitchen table. 'Will this help, Leigh?' he asked. Just like that. Would you believe he'd saved all his prize money? And most of his wages. For his old age, he said. But I guess he figured investing in the stables would do more for his future. So now he and I are partners. Howdy, pardner," she whooped as Ed chose that moment to appear.

Freshly splashed with shaving lotion, slick-combed and wearing a blue shirt with a string tie, he looked younger and quite unlike himself. He didn't talk much during dinner. Michael concentrated on winding long strands of spaghetti around his fork and Tracy was feeling too glum to make pleasant conversation, so Leigh did most of the talking.

When they'd started on dessert, however—stemmed glasses filled with lemon and lime sherbet—Tracy decided to tell them about the spray-painting job someone had done on her shop. She didn't enjoy talking about it in front of Ed, but she couldn't hold back any longer.

"My guess is Suzanne did it," Leigh blurted out.

"Oh, Leigh," Tracy sighed. "You'd blame her for the Chicago fire if you could figure a way to place her on the scene. I mean, she's not my favorite person, either, but—"

"She's got a vicious streak a mile wide. And she hates me."

"Leigh, it just doesn't make sense. Can you imagine Miss Fashion Plate breaking her fingernails on a can of spray paint? Or taking the risk of getting caught in the act? Anyway, if she wanted to get at you, why smear me? Why not just practice her graffiti on the side of the house?"

Leigh cackled, rubbing her hands together. "Oh, I wish she'd try!"

Tracy hadn't mentioned the incident with Suzanne the day before. And she didn't mention it now. She decided to ignore her own feelings of disquiet, evoked by the memory of Suzanne's sudden rage. "Let's not talk about it anymore," she said quickly, pushing back her chair. "The sheriff has been notified. I don't think it'll happen again."

She felt relieved that Leigh was willing to drop the subject—and even more relieved that Ed seemed too involved in his conversation with Michael to pay them any attention.

"You're right. Talking about Suzanne is a good way to spoil anything," Leigh muttered as she started to collect the dessert glasses. "And I worked too hard over this dinner to have it spoiled."

"Which exempts you from the dishes, by the way. I'll wash." Tracy fastened an eye on her brother. "Do I hear anybody volunteering to dry?"

When the kitchen had been tidied, Tracy changed into her red Western-style shirt. Leigh and Michael settled down to their usual fight-to-the-death game of checkers. Ed sat at the desk going over bills and Willie went to sleep in front of the refrigerator, not wanting to miss snack time when it came around.

"You aren't going riding, are you?" Leigh asked Tracy. "It looks like rain."

"I've gotten into the habit. It helps me unwind. Believe me, I need it after today."

"Don't take Roxy then. She gets spooked by thunder."

"Aw, how can I hurt her feelings? She looks forward to our nightly meanderings as much as I do. Don't worry. I'll head back if it looks like it'll turn into a downpour."

The trail she followed was the one she always chose. An old Indian trail, people said. It narrowed and dipped beneath a wide overhang of rock and might have painfully surprised an unwary rider, who wasn't prepared to crouch low after the descent.

It wound steeply upward then and found its way at last to the top of the same ledge. Here she dismounted and reveled in the idea that she could look down at the soaring flight of birds, at the surrounding green of the land, at houses, corrals and squared-off patches of lush farmland. There, below, was Ryle's land. Ryle's land. It sounded like the title of an old Western movie.

Why did she play these tricks on herself? Why did she pretend she was doing her darnedest to forget Ryle, and then stand up here, as she'd stood the night before, looking down at his house? Was she hoping, as a starry-eyed child might, to catch a glimpse of him from afar? Was she even considering the possibility that he might see her, mount his own horse and like the Sheikh of Araby, ride up after her and sweep her into his arms?

She sighed. The trees looked like a solid mass of blue in the distance. The smell of woodsmoke played at the edges of her memory, recalling the long-ago fires. She rubbed her arms. The sky to the west was unnaturally bright, but to the north, blackish clouds had formed and were swirling toward her.

Time to head back.

The way down was steeper, but no danger to a horse and rider who picked their way with care. She reined Roxy under control and spoke to her gently when the first spear of lightning lit up the sky and thunder rumbled. Then there was another flash. And another. The rain was coming in large warm drops. Soon those drops came faster and faster. She urged Roxy onward, but clearly the animal was beginning to panic. The sky was now almost completely dark.

"It's all right, girl," she tried. "There's my Roxy. There."

But the animal didn't respond. A spill of rocks had been washed across the path and the ground had already become slick and treacherous. Repeatedly the horse lost her footing. They would have to dig in somewhere—quick—and wait out the worst of the storm. The nearest place was . . . Ryle's house.

He wasn't home. But there was a light on in his living room and his back door was unlocked. She stabled Roxy, then dashed into Ryle's kitchen to use his telephone.

"Thank God you're all right!" Leigh cried when Tracy called and told her where they were.

"Ryle isn't here. But I'm sure he won't mind. I've fixed Roxy up warm and comfortable in the barn and she's quieted down."

"Whew! This weather's gone crazy. I can't remember when we've had a rain this bad. I was so worried about you! Don't even think of trying to get home in this, okay? Stay where you are until morning."

"I plan to. I'll see you when I can. And Leigh—thanks."

Tracy dug a couple of bath towels out of the jumble of unfolded wash in the laundry basket sitting on the kitchen table. She rubbed herself dry with one, and wrapped a second, turban-style, around her head. She slid a couple of flannel blankets off a closet shelf, looked around to make sure everything was exactly as she'd found it, and went out to keep Roxy company. With a little luck, her host wouldn't even know she'd been there.

CHAPTER SEVEN

WHEN THE DOOR CRASHED OPEN, Tracy thought the storm had blown the roof off. She burst out of sleep to sit upright, her heart beating triple time. Then she saw Ryle. Only a dark shape in the doorway until a flash of lightning showed that he was naked to the waist, barefoot and dripping.

"Tracy?"

"What is it?" she asked, trying for a show of dignity, despite the circumstances.

"What the hell are you doing? I wouldn't even have known you were here if Leigh hadn't called to check on you."

"I'm fine."

"I'm fine," he mimicked in an unflattering high-pitched voice.

"Yes. I was asleep. I didn't want to disturb you."

He snorted. "Always so damned considerate, aren't you? Hiding out here in the barn like a shivering little field mouse. Come on. Hightail it into the house."

"I'm comfortable where I am. The hay is as soft as a mattress. This way I won't have to disturb you when I leave in the morning."

"You've already disturbed me. That wasn't a request, Whelan. Get off your butt." The harshness in his voice warned her that he almost hoped she'd challenge him.

She snuggled back in the hay and pulled the blanket more tightly about her. "You're being unreasonable and I haven't taken orders for years."

"You will when you're trespassing on my turf." He lunged toward her, seizing her wrist with his fingers and yanking her easily to her feet. "Come on."

Shoving her in front of him and into the blinding rain, he latched the barn door, then made for the house, still holding her fast. Twice she almost lost her balance, and only sheer anger kept her from falling.

"Does this make sense?" she raged at him when they were inside. "I was perfectly dry. Now look at me."

"Here." He wadded up a striped pajama top and tossed it at her. "Get out of those clothes while I call Leigh and tell her I found you."

"It's late. You'll wake her."

"Do you imagine she's sleeping? She was frantic when I told her you weren't here. You put people who care about you through hell, don't you? You never give a thought to anyone but yourself, do you?"

It was an accusation not worth answering. "Let me talk to her."

He turned his back, holding the telephone up high so that she couldn't reach it while he explained the situation to Leigh, hunching his shoulders and turning away as Tracy moved around him. Finally, she gave up and used his inattention to slip out of her wet clothes and into the oversize pajama top.

"Right," he was saying. "I'll lock her in the broom closet if necessary. See you tomorrow."

"I'd like to see you get even a child-size broom into that utility closet of yours," Tracy snapped. "It's packed from floor to ceiling."

"Tsk, tsk. You've been peeking."

"I was looking for something to sleep on."

"Try the bed." He brought a towel out of the bathroom and began to briskly rub her hair. She felt the movement of his strong supple fingers and for a moment, she was tempted to succumb to their dangerous pressure, tempted to relax and accept what he was offering. Then the image of Leigh intervened. Leigh, worrying, waiting by the phone. Leigh, who trusted her. She suddenly tensed, jerking her head forward, and tried to wrest the towel away from him. But he casually brushed her hands aside, then went on drying her hair.

"Simmer down, Whelan," he said in a quiet voice.

"Why should I? You behaved like a jerk. An overbearing, pompous jerk."

"You're right. I did. I didn't mean to jump on you. You just scared me. Okay?"

She drew a deep breath. "Okay."

"I'll spread your wet things on the back of this chair. They'll be dry in the morning."

"Spread your own clothes on the back of the chair," she said, taking her underthings away from him. They looked like flimsy wisps of nothing in his hands. "I'll take care of these myself, thank you."

"Did you just ask me to undress?"

"I did not!" She laughed in spite of herself.

"I could have sworn you told me to take off my clothes and put them on the back of that chair. Oh, well." He slung the towel he'd used to dry her hair over his shoulder. "Would you like me to build a fire?"

"We don't need one."

"You're right. We don't." His eyes slid over her face, caressing it. "It's one hell of a rain, all right. But it's an ill wind that brings no good."

"What does that mean?"

"It means I have you prisoner. We'll be here together—all night—with no interruptions. You have no choice but to talk to me."

"Don't start in, Ryle." She took a deep, steadying breath. "The only thing we have to talk about is sleeping arrangements."

"That's the one thing we won't need to talk about."

To distract both of them from the turn the conversation had taken, Tracy looked frantically around the room. Her eyes settled on the wood bin by the door. Ryle's shoes sat in it. His good shoes. They were soaked and covered with dark, sticky mud. "You must have been caught in the storm before you came out to the barn looking for me."

"I was. I'd only dried myself off when Leigh called."

"Two drenchings in one night. At least they weren't both on my account—were they?"

"Don't presume too much, Whelan." He raked the towel from his shoulder and let it drop onto a chair. His eyebrow peaked. Tracy knew what that look meant; he was getting ready to make his move.

"You should clean them now—your shoes. Don't let them dry that way." She couldn't help her nervous chatter.

"Morning will be soon enough."

Morning. The word struck a discordant note. "They'll be ruined."

"Give less thought to the shoes, woman," he said, in a voice that was supposed to sound like either W.C. Fields or Groucho Marx. "And more to the man. Sit down."

"Shouldn't we try to get some sleep?"

"Later. Sit down. Please."

Inhaling sharply, she cleared a space on the couch, picking up a stack of *Farm World* magazines and setting them neatly on the floor. Then she sat down. "All right," she announced, "I'm sitting."

"Usually a woman only has to tell me 'no' once," he said. "She doesn't get another chance."

"Then..."

He raised a flat palm to silence her. "I spent a lot of hard time blaming you for our breakup. Then you came back and asked me a good question. Why hadn't I fought to keep you? Why hadn't I let you know how much you mattered to me? I thought it over and came to the conclusion that maybe you were right. So I'm fighting this time."

"Ryle..."

He held up the hand again. "One last time. One supreme effort to sort this mess out."

Tracy pressed her fingers to the bridge of her nose to still the throbbing that had begun there. It didn't help. "What do you want to talk about?"

"Let's not rush this. First a glass of wine. It'll warm you."

She needed no wine for that. But she didn't say so. She didn't even like wine. But she didn't say that, either. The room fell silent as he left to get the bottle and the glasses, stumbling over the wastebasket in the process.

Tracy huddled in her corner of the sofa and glanced idly about the room. It looked a little less chaotic than it had at the time of her last visit—at least the laundry had been picked up. The coffee table was as cluttered as before. She noticed again the chamois pouch with its catlinite. The medical dictionary and the old photograph propped against it. The envelope filled with high school snapshots.

Tracy grimaced as she reached for it and riffled quickly through the pictures. Half-ashamed, she slipped them back into their envelope. She could hear Ryle, still rummaging in kitchen cupboards, running water, opening drawers. For just a few seconds, she allowed herself to think of the future she might have had with him—if things had turned out differently. But they hadn't, and she'd do well to remember that.

Her hand wandered, seemingly of its own accord, to the soft tan pouch. She shook the stones into her open palm and closed her hand tightly, feeling their smooth coolness against her skin. She was staring at the reddish stones, moving her hand to watch the way their polished surfaces gleamed in the light, when Ryle walked in.

"Ah, the stones. You couldn't resist them, could you? You're thinking of the night of the Spring Moon, and the two of us going out to bury these stones. Together."

Clumsily, she slid them back into the pouch and tossed it on the table. "What I'm thinking, Tanner, is that I could really use some sleep. In fact, I'm so damn tired I could sleep for a year—right past your precious night of the Spring Moon." She faked a yawn.

He chuckled and she felt the familiar rush of pleasure and longing at the sound.

"Here you go, Rip van Whelan." He filled her wineglass and handed it to her. Then he filled his own.

Tracy leaned back on the couch, her legs curled under her. Taking an occasional sip of the wine, she watched him shift books and boxes to make room for himself beside her. And she listened as he spoke calmly and earnestly about emotional scars and trauma. The steady fall of the rain, punctuated now and then by a deafening thunderclap, merged with the sound of his voice. Not knowing that the barrier between them lay in the present, he could only imagine it came from the past. She must have been deeply hurt by someone, he said. Perhaps it went back to the business with Scott. Perhaps it was because of the man she'd almost married. If only she could talk about it, he told her, it would help.

The man she'd almost married. It seemed so long ago. She could barely remember what he looked like, what they'd talked about. The disappointment she'd felt about breaking off the engagement had faded quickly and been replaced by a sense of relief. What they had shared, she realized now, was nothing compared to what she shared with Ryle. What she had lost was nothing to what she would lose when Ryle was gone from her life.

"I want you to know that I don't mind waiting," he was saying. "I only need to know one thing. Is there a reason for me to wait?"

"Oh, Ryle," she cried, her voice no more than a sigh as she reached out to him. It was going to happen for them tonight. Just once. But never again, God help her.

He took her glass with trembling fingers and put it carefully beside his own on the low table. He might have been performing some ritual action, some ceremonial prelude, for the tension that surrounded his movements.

Gripping her shoulders as much to steady himself as to steady her, he took her mouth with his, as though he had never taken it before. And he hadn't. Not like this.

Though his kiss brought with it a numbing pleasure, it wasn't born of lust. Its demands wouldn't be soothed when the physical body was satisfied. It was a kiss that demanded total surrender.

Her feet were no longer on the floor. Her arms were around his neck and he was carrying her into the bedroom, kicking obstacles aside as he went. The springs creaked as his body weighed hers heavily into the mattress and continued its telltale creaking as his mouth, still hot and moist, returned to hers again until every inch of her prickled with delight.

His lips, his teeth, his tongue, were here and there, and there again. All the while his hands were methodically exploring the soft curves and gentle hollows of her body and making them his. She was aware of a hazy glow from the hall light and shadowy corners. Nothing more.

"I love you so very much," she whispered, surprising herself not so much with the words, but with the intensity of her feeling. She had to say it now, even if she was forced to deny it in the morning.

His stomach muscles knotted as he burrowed his face against her neck. "Oh, honey," he murmured. "If only you knew how much I've wanted to hear you say that. Nothing else matters. Nothing."

Cool air skimmed over her as his hold on her relaxed. He was studying her with the kind of awe that might have shown in the face of an artist as he looked at his most cherished work—and it made her feel cherished.

A soft padding brought the pit bull to the bedside. The dog whined softly and pressed its nose against Ryle's leg.

"You're absolutely right, boy," Ryle said with a sigh.

"What did he say?"

"He said—it's time I got out of here and let you sleep."

"What does he know?"

"Oh, he's a wise old codger. He's been around." Ryle slid a hand lovingly along the line of her hip and eased himself away. "We're not going to make love tonight, Tracy."

When her lips formed a protest, he bent over again, to stop it with a brief, hard kiss. "Maybe I'm a prize fool—probably—but what we have here is too precious to waste. I don't want us to make love just because you were running away from a rainstorm. I want it to be thought out and perfect to the smallest detail. Do you understand?"

She nodded.

"Then I wish you'd explain it to me." He stood up in slow motion, as if the act were physically painful. "I'd like to stretch out beside you, at least, and hold you in my arms all night. I'd like to watch you as you sleep and kiss you awake. But I'm not strong enough to manage that." He jerked his head toward the living room and grimaced. "So, it's the couch for me tonight."

She nodded again, feeling a burning in her eyes.

"Aren't you going to talk me out of it?" he asked.

"No. Because you're right."

"Fine time for you to start agreeing with me."

"Good night, Tanner," she said softly.

"Good night, Whelan."

THE NEXT MORNING, she and Ryle worked together, preparing breakfast, getting in each other's way at sink and stove, and settling the blame with intimate pats and warm kisses. Together they ate, and together they washed the dishes and put things in their proper places—when such places could be decided upon. Ryle's conception of "place" was any bare spot—as if he were setting together a giant jigsaw puzzle whose pieces could be interchanged to create a new puzzle picture each day.

Together they walked to the barn, hand in hand, and cold reality moved with them, bringing a sadness that weighed Tracy down. It was time for the parting. And worse, for the words, if she could find them, that would make the parting permanent.

"There's no need for you to ride along," she told him, summoning her Bette Davis voice again, when he'd saddled Roxy and was about to do the same with Mikapi. "I think I can find my way home."

He hunched his shoulders and squinted at her. His eyes looked amber in the early-morning light. "Well...I should run out to Jim Grayson's before I check in with Doc Cole at the office."

"Do that, doc." She offered him a crisp smile and a firm hand. "Thank you for last night."

He looked blankly at the hand, but didn't take it. "Anytime, sport. Aren't we formal this morning?"

"Mornings are usually a bit awkward, aren't they?"

"Are they?"

She stroked Roxy lovingly, then led her into the yard. Ryle followed several steps behind, not saying anything. She was glad. It was difficult to look at him without showing her true feelings. She took a deep breath. "Let's not make it any more awkward than it has to be."

"Don't turn screwball on me again, Tracy." The words were spoken through clenched teeth. "I wouldn't appreciate it."

"Night is night and day is day."

"Is that supposed to be like 'never the twain shall meet'?"

"In a roundabout way, yes."

"If this is your daytime personality, I don't like it."

"Sorry, doc. But this is me."

"Don't call me 'doc'. And last night. What was that?"

The rising heat of the day was already beginning to erase signs of last night's storm. The ground was steamy. By midday there would be dust.

"Nothing happened between us last night, thanks to you, and I'm relieved," she began. "Don't misunderstand me. We would have been good together. There's a kind of chemistry at work here, isn't there? I couldn't help wanting to... well, see what it would be like.'' She shriveled inside, embarrassed at the uncharacteristic nakedness of her words.

Ryle took a few steps away from her and rocked back and forth on his heels. "Are you actually saying..." He laughed, but his lips were colorless and taut. "I seem to recall your saying you loved me. Is that just something you tell guys when you want their bodies? If that's the case, I'm sorry you were cheated.''

"I am, too. I think you would be an exciting lover.''

"What kind of rating do you think you'd give me on a scale of one to ten?''

"We'll never know, will we?'' She tried to sound off-hand. "I'm sorry if I've made you feel used. It's what men have always done, isn't it? Used women?''

"I never have. There has to be something here—and here.'' He jabbed a finger at his forehead, then his chest. "If there isn't, all the rest of it is just yesterday's news.''

She allowed her eyes to roam over the length and breadth of him appreciatively. "I can't believe you're so naive. Maybe you spend too much time with your patients to know what's going on in the real world.''

"If I thought this nonsense you're spouting was really you, I could walk away without a glance over my shoulder. Tracy, there aren't good and bad lovers as such. Technique doesn't count for a damn if people don't care about each other. And if people don't care about each other, it doesn't matter if...'' He shook his head in frustration. "You're making me tongue-tied. Forget it.''

"Ryle, you—''

"I know. I'd be a terrific lover. Can I count on a good reference from you, then?''

Tracy swung herself into the saddle. "Yesterday was a nightmare for me—the graffiti and everything. You helped me to survive it.''

"Now I'm your therapist.''

"In a sense. I hope we can still be friends.''

"You don't know the meaning of the word 'friend.'" For one frightening moment, his face was transformed by anger and contempt, the face of a stranger.

"I'm sorry you feel like that," she said quietly.

"Stay out of my way," he snarled, giving her horse a swat on the rump. "I'm warning you."

CHAPTER EIGHT

"WHAT DO YOU THINK?" Leigh posed in the doorway, her coppery hair curled and side parted, her bangs swept off her high forehead. It was a longer imitation of Tracy's own hairdo.

"I like the new softness." Tracy was grateful for the opportunity to offer advice on her friend's appearance. She had to tread carefully though. Leigh was hypersensitive to criticism. "But there's so much of it. Why don't I trim the ends tonight?"

Leigh's shoulders sagged. It wasn't the answer she had wanted. "Too late."

"Tonight's too late? I presume you're expecting Prince Charming to materialize before then?"

"You've got it. Ryle will be around to take a look at the pony this afternoon sometime, and I thought I'd floor him with a new and irresistible look."

"Some Prince Charming! Ugh!" Michael let his spoon splash back into his Cheerios. "He thinks he knows everything just because he's a pet doctor. But he doesn't know anything. He only knows how to take care of animals."

"I didn't mean I don't like your hair that way," Tracy tried again. "If you'd—"

"Never mind." Leigh turned toward the sink and began rinsing the coffee cups. "It was a stupid idea."

"I like your hair better in a horse's tail," Michael told her.

"That's me," she said. "The tail end of a horse."

"Michael, you're only playing with that spoon," Tracy said quickly, pretending she hadn't heard what Leigh said.

"You've obviously had enough. We'd better go. See you later, Leigh." She grabbed Michael's arm and hurried him out to the car.

It was best not to react when Leigh was putting herself down, Tracy thought as she backed out of the driveway. Besides, a new hairdo was in the future for Leigh. The very near future—maybe that very evening, if Tracy could talk her into it.

"Don't forget to come home early," Michael said, hesitating before he got out of the car in the school parking lot. "Willie has to be at Garfield Park at five-thirty."

Willie, who was with them, heard his name and began dancing around on the car seat.

"Sit down, boy," Tracy scolded. "Since when does Willie have appointments?"

"The dog obedience class. Doc Tanner's giving it. You know. There's gonna be ten lessons and a medal for the best dog at the end of it. I told you."

"This is the first I've heard of it. You must have told Leigh. Besides, I thought you didn't even like Ryle Tanner. I thought you said he didn't know anything."

"Aw, you know. He's okay with dogs. And I wanna show him how smart Willie is. I wanna show everybody. Willie's gonna win first prize."

"Forget it, Michael. Willie's too old to learn new things. You know what they say."

"Dave's dog is only two years younger and he's in it. He's just this big dumb old basset hound. It only costs eighteen dollars."

"Eighteen dollars? Do you suppose I can snap my fingers and produce the money? Things are tight right now."

"Willie's worth it, isn't he?" The boy scampered away, but was back before she could turn the car around. "I almost forgot. Mrs. Campbell wants to see you."

She groaned. "What did you do now?"

"Nothing. I didn't do nothing."

When the teacher closed the classroom door before speaking, Tracy prepared herself for the worst. But it was all right. The end-of-school picnic was the day after tomorrow. Could she volunteer to help some of the mothers supervise the children at the fairgrounds?

"If you can fit it into your schedule," the woman said, "I think it would be good for Michael to have you there. And it would be very helpful to me. Besides, you'll have a perfectly delightful time."

Tracy was surprised to hear herself agreeing. Contrary to the teacher's opinion, her idea of a delightful time wasn't playing mother hen to a flock of feisty fourth- and fifth-graders. But she'd been so relieved to hear that Michael wasn't in trouble, she would have agreed to anything.

As she turned into the alley, she was mentally kicking herself for not being quick-witted enough to think of an excuse to get out of baby-sitting Michael and his classmates. She hardly noticed the furtive movement at the back door of the shop until she saw someone running. It was a boy of about seventeen or eighteen, wearing a striped tank top and a baseball cap. By the time she'd brought the car to a stop, he'd disappeared around the corner. She scrambled out and ran in pursuit, reaching the corner just in time to see a black car screech away from the curb. It was too old and battered for her to recognize its make, and the license plate was too mud spattered, probably by intent, for her to see the numbers. But she saw two other people in the car besides the one who ran.

Almost afraid to look, she hurried back to the shop. Raw eggs had been hurled against the iron grillwork of the windows, but there was no real damage that she could see. The note that had been fastened to the door with a dart held a simple message. Go Home, Pyro.

"Super," she muttered to herself as she hosed the windows down. At least eggs were easier to deal with than paint.

She set Willie in the back room with a bowl of water, a chew bone and a few words of praise. Then she closed the bottom half of the Dutch door to keep him from having the run of the shop while she went about her work.

Ed had removed a section of the backyard fence to repair it and she'd had to bring Willie along to prevent him from escaping. Now she was grateful for the four-legged company. The little face that always seemed to be smiling and the forever-wagging tail seemed to be the only signs of optimism around.

Less than fifteen minutes later, two men arrived in a truck with an unexpected delivery. New chairs, and the dryers to go with them. While she was arguing that there had been a mistake, the bell sounded over the front door again.

"That clanging!" Suzanne complained, letting her handbag drop onto the counter. "It sounds like a cowbell. Maybe you can order chimes that play 'Beautiful Lady' or something."

Tracy planted a fist on each hipbone and shook her head.

"What's going on here? Do you know anything about all this?"

Suzanne's blue eyes were wide and innocent. "How would I know anything? I just got here."

"My point exactly," Tracy said wryly. "Look—the order says 'Barclay' in black and white. How do you explain that?"

"Well, I'm not the only Barclay in town, am I? Obviously Daddy Dearest wanted to present his lady with a surprise gift."

"We all know that's nonsense. Now what's the real reason?"

"I think Daddy Dearest knows a beautiful woman when he sees one."

"And I think you're being ridiculous."

"Maybe he heard about your vandals and feels sorry for you."

"Oh? Who told him? You?"

"Don't be silly," the girl replied coolly. "In a town like this, everyone knows everything."

Tracy sighed. "I suppose so. But I can't accept such a present from him for *any* reason."

"Ladies," one of the moving men said with exaggerated politeness, "will one of you sign for this stuff?"

"Uncrate it first," Suzanne said.

"But she told me not to." He jabbed a thumb at Tracy.

"Uncrate it. Please." Suzanne favored him with one of her most beguiling smiles.

"No!" Tracy objected.

The man dropped his arms to his sides and rolled his eyes toward the ceiling. "This is going to be one of those days."

"If I know my father, he'll be here momentarily," Suzanne promised, without letting her smile slip a notch. "He'll make the waiting worth your while."

"Five minutes, lady. No more." The man looked at his watch. "Have a smoke, if you want, Hayes," he barked at his assistant.

"Outside, if you don't mind? The odor?" Suzanne snatched up her handbag. "I'll be going. Don't want Daddy to catch me loitering. Let me know how all this comes out."

Tracy stopped her. "Why do you put so much effort into hiding? How terrible can your job be?"

"It's degrading beyond description. I'm expected to spend my time collecting tidbits of social gossip and penning the 'What's Happening in Council Grove' column. As if anything is happening in this town."

"Well, why did you take the job if you think it's so degrading?"

"Remember I told you how Daddy arranged for the editor to hire me? Well he *made* me take the job. To get back at me for dropping out of college in the middle of the semester."

"What do you want to do?"

"I want to write. But not that drivel."

"Then quit. Strike out on your own."

"Why should I have to?" The girl's eyes flashed and the fury Tracy had seen at the stables came back into them again. "My father is loaded. Would Scotty have to make it on his own if he were alive? No. Daddy would have backed him in whatever he wanted to do. Why not me, too? He always gave Scotty everything. What's he ever given me?" She gestured at the crates. "And now look! He's giving you things and you're not even family. It's so unfair and—Yikes!" She slapped at Tracy's arm and made a dash for the other room. "Here he comes. I told you."

"Not that way," Tracy called after her. But it was too late. Suzanne had gone into the room with Willie. The only way out was a door that had been unused for a long time and was nailed shut.

Howard Barclay signed the delivery order, gave the men some money and directed them to begin the uncrating with such brisk authority that Tracy didn't have a chance to open her mouth. He took her arm and led her to one side. "Let's stay clear and let them work."

"These things will have to be returned, Mr. Barclay. If you won't see to it, I'll do it myself when you've gone."

"You know very well your shop can't succeed with such shabby equipment."

"I'm depending on my skill as a stylist to bring me customers."

"It may keep them coming, dear, but it won't bring them here in the first place."

"And new dryers will?"

"You know it as well as I do—or you wouldn't have put this much effort into fixing up the place. Image. That's what counts. And the right atmosphere; you've got to make your customers feel pampered." They watched as the men finished setting up the new chairs and removing the old ones. Howard didn't go on arguing with Tracy, but stood silently beside her, giving her time, waiting for her to fall in love with her new look.

And fall in love with it she did. Everything was pink and white and gold. The chairs made all the difference. Only in her imagination had her salon looked so elegant, so dramatic, and then it had always been "someday."

Howard took her hand. His grasp was warm and eager. "You like them. I can tell. And you deserve them, Tracy. I want you to know I admire your courage. You came back here after that mess ten years ago. And you have the strength of character to stick it out, even after my... after you were vandalized."

"How did you find out about that?"

"To be honest, I've been keeping an eye on you, because I'm concerned that—" He raised a hand to forestall Tracy's protests. "Don't be offended, please. Just let me do this one thing for you. Let's just say it's in memory of Scott." His voice was hoarse with emotion. "When I lost him, I lost everything that truly mattered to me."

"You have a daughter," she reminded him gently.

"Suzanne, hah!" He snorted so explosively, Tracy wished she hadn't said anything. It was probable the girl had heard, trapped as she was in the other room. "She's a frivolous, spoiled brat, without a brain in her head. She hasn't got a fraction of the character you've got. Thinks she has a right to anything she wants—always buying more expensive clothes, or standing in front of a mirror, admiring herself in the ones she already has."

"Maybe if you took more time to know her—"

"I know her."

A crash and then another from the back room turned his head. He frowned. "What the deuce was that?"

"I brought my dog today," she told him, attempting a smile. "He isn't used to being confined."

Tracy wondered how Suzanne had reacted to her father's chilling appraisal. She felt a surge of pity for them both, the grieving, misguided man and the daughter he couldn't seem to love. Granted, Suzanne wasn't particularly lovable, but Tracy had read enough basic psychology to guess that at least some of the blame must have been Howard's. Yet she knew there wasn't a thing she could say or do to make him see that.

She suddenly realized that he had said something to her and that he expected an answer. "Pardon, Howard?"

"I said, so, you'll accept the new chairs and dryers."

"I will. If I can pay you for them."

"Does a dollar a month sound about right?"

She smiled. "I can do better than that. But I'd appreciate it if you'd wait until September for the first installment."

"Make it the first of the year." He stopped at the door. "The place looks good, Tracy. You're going to do well here." He gave her a jaunty salute.

As soon as he'd gone, Tracy sped to the other room and threw the door open, trying to think of something she might say to Suzanne.

"Darn!" The alley door was ajar. Suzanne had managed to pry away the nails and make her escape. Willie hadn't ignored his opportunity to do the same.

After securing the shop, she moved down the alley, calling the dog's name. At the end of the second block, a trash can was overturned and its contents spilled. Willie's modus operandi. But he was nowhere in sight.

Where would he go? Would he tire and return to the shop? Or would he be too befuddled in these unfamiliar surroundings to find the shop again?

The park? Maybe.

Voices caught her attention. A small knot of people were gathered at the curb near the historical marker. Her stomach cramped. What if Willie had been hit by a car?

It wasn't the dog. It was a boy. He was sitting on the sidewalk, nursing a scraped knee. "It's her dog did it." He pointed.

Everyone looked at Tracy.

"Why don't you keep him chained up?" a man asked. "This kid fell off his bike trying to keep from hitting him. The stupid mutt ran right in front of him."

"I'm sorry. He got out by accident. Are you okay?"

The boy inspected his leg. "I guess. But my wheel's bent."

"Have it fixed and I'll pay for it," she told him. "Thanks for dodging Willie. Do you know where he is?"

"Somebody took him over to Doc Tanner's."

Ryle. That was all she needed.

He was sitting on the edge of the front desk when she walked into his office. She swallowed hard, recognizing the narrowed eye and the rigid set of his jaw. She knew what that meant.

She didn't give him the chance to say a word. Immediately she launched into her defense, telling him about having to bring Willie to work, about having a visitor who left the back door open and about the dog's escape. "May I have him now?"

Ryle took a notepad and scribbled something. When he'd finished, he tore off the top sheet and thrust it at her.

Was he so angry he planned to resort to notes instead of speaking? She tried to read what it said, but the handwriting was illegible. Only a word or two stood out. A date, a time and his signature.

"What is this?"

"A citation. For allowing an animal to run loose in town."

She glared at him. The top button was missing from his green sport shirt and he looked as if he'd combed his hair with his fingers. "You have the authority to do this, I presume?"

"I have. It was my idea. Duly presented and accepted at the town meeting. It's worked very well."

"But I explained to you that Willie's getting out was an accident."

"That doesn't let you off the hook. You run a business. You'll have people going in and out all day. It's up to you to see that your pet is safe."

"What does it mean? Is there a large fine?"

"No fine at all. You'll have to attend a lecture and film on responsible pet ownership. The date is there. It's the first Monday of next month."

"A lecture given by you?"

"Me or Doc Cole. Whoever's available." He ran a finger under a line of writing at the bottom of the sheet. He was close to her now. She could detect the heady scent of whatever soap he used. It brought back memories of the night before. She saw the medallion too, resting comfortably against the scattering of amber hair on his chest, where her head had rested not so many hours before. His arm brushed against hers and he shifted his weight. Now the steamy heat of his body touched hers. She forced herself to ignore it.

"I'm grateful to you for deciphering this chicken scratching for me," she said, looking at the paper again. "You know this is ridiculous."

"Not at all. Animal-related accidents have dropped off remarkably since we began this program."

"I thought maybe you'd dreamed it up for my benefit."

"You would think that, wouldn't you?"

Tracy didn't want to fight with him. He'd been hurt. In his eyes, she had treated him unconscionably. If possible, she would retreat from his anger and allow it to die naturally. But he obviously wasn't going to make it easy for her. The air was electrically charged with the tension between them.

"I'm new in town, doc. Don't strangers usually get off with a warning for a first offense?"

"You had your warning, lady. The day you drove into town and left Willie to roast in your car."

"I see." She drew a quick breath and stuffed the ticket into her handbag. "And if I don't come to this lecture?"

"The sheriff will send someone after you."

"With handcuffs?"

"I like to think so."

"Maybe you might suggest revival of the ducking stool and the stocks."

"It's a thought."

She fastened her eyes on his, wanting to force him to look away first. He didn't. His lips twitched with satisfaction. "I might as well give you the eighteen dollars for Willie's obedience training while I'm here. The lessons were Michael's idea."

"That doesn't surprise me. You aren't gung ho on obedience for dogs *or* kids."

"Would you like to explain what you mean by that?"

"I think it's self-explanatory."

She dug into her purse, though she could tell at first glance that her wallet wasn't there. Michael had needed change. She'd taken out her wallet and left it on the kitchen table. "I'll have to give you the money tonight."

"Forget it." His smile was too wide to be genuine. And it didn't reach his eyes. "I'll let you have the lessons in exchange for the services you rendered last night." His gaze rolled over the length of her, tearing away her clothing, letting the meaning of his offer sink in. "It wasn't your fault I didn't get full value."

She blinked. "Eighteen dollars."

"Give or take a buck. I like to be generous."

"What's the penalty for slapping a self-styled humane officer across his smug face?"

His expression didn't change. "It isn't official, but I don't think you'd like it."

"May I have my dog now?" She snapped her handbag closed and slung the strap over her shoulder.

"Take him."

"Thank you."

"Tracy?"

"Yes?"

"If you take that dog outside without a leash, I'll cite you again."

She growled under her breath, "I don't have a leash with me. What am I supposed to do?"

He pretended to be busy with some paperwork. "Carry him. Just be thankful."

"For what?"

"Willie could have been a great dane."

CHAPTER NINE

THE DAY HADN'T BEEN one to wash away with a brisk shower. Tracy had earned a luxuriant soak and she would have it. Michael had eaten his dinner early and was now rehearsing Willie for his appearance in the obedience class. Leigh was shopping. An entire hour was hers before she had to think about Garfield Park and the parade of canine students.

With her hair pulled into a rubber band, Leigh-fashion, she stepped into the tub, immersed herself in slow motion and allowed the warm water to close over her.

Four sharp knocks announced someone at the bathroom door. "Trace, are you in there?"

She groaned. Leigh was back early. "I'm taking a bath."

"Hurry up, will you? I have something to show you."

Leigh was in her bedroom, eyes dancing with expectancy. Two fancy cowboy shirts lay on the bed. "Which do you like better?"

"For this you got me out of my tub?" Tracy brushed her hair back with rising impatience, wondering who was the most childlike—her brother or her friend. "Aren't they awfully big for you?"

Leigh giggled. "They're for Ryle, silly. For the barn dance. My own personal choice would be the rust and yellow. Can't you see that terrific mane of hair and those dreamy brown eyes with the autumn colors in that shirt? But men like blue best, don't they?"

"Since when do you buy Ryle's clothes?"

"Shh!" Leigh pressed a finger to her lips. "He's outside, doing a follow-up on the pony's indigestion. I told you this morning."

"I thought he'd been here and gone."

"I invited him in after, for a bacon and tomato sandwich. In this, our ever-changing universe, one thing remains constant. Ryle Tanner will not turn down a bacon and tomato sandwich. So—when he comes in, I present him with his shirt as a thanks for all the—"

"No."

"His birthday is next month."

"No."

"But if I give it to him, what can he do but accept when I ask him to be my partner for the barn dance? Not my date, exactly—more like a cohost. First and last waltz. And all the ones in between if I can manage it."

"Return the shirts. Both of them." Tracy picked up her towel again and headed back to her warm tub. "It isn't a good idea."

"Are you sure?"

"Positive. In fact, it's a terrible idea. An atrocious one."

It wasn't long before the smell of bacon touched her nostrils. She could hear Leigh in the kitchen, laughing. Much as Tracy had craved her long soak, now she felt trapped. She wouldn't be able to get out until Ryle had gone.

She could imagine the scene. Ryle at the table. Leigh flitting around, flirting with him, toasting bread, slicing tomatoes and spreading mayonnaise for his sandwich. He would be resting his elbows on the table, touching his fingertips together as he waited. Perhaps he'd be joking in the slow, easy way he had, saying outlandish things so earnestly the humor of them didn't sink in immediately. Or maybe he'd be discouraged about his day. Or thoughtful. He'd get that hazy faraway look that never failed to make her want to hold him close, even if part of her still wanted to wring his neck.

"You're going to come out of the water all white and wrinkly," Leigh called at last.

"Are you alone?" Tracy wanted to know.

"Couldn't I just tell Ryle that the shirt is to make up for all the times he waited for his money when my folks and I couldn't afford to pay?"

Good, thought Tracy. He was gone.

"Do whatever you like," Tracy answered, exasperated now as she rubbed herself dry.

"Are you sure you aren't speaking out of prejudice? You don't like Ryle. He told me about the citation. But you shouldn't take it personally. He tickets everybody."

"I'm not prejudiced against him."

"Maybe without realizing it you resent men in general. You don't seem too crazy about Ed, either. And then that guy you were going to marry—you broke off with him. Do you think, maybe, your, um, unfortunate experience with Scott could have made you—you know—bitter?"

"And now I gleefully want to deprive Ryle of a shirt."

"I'd say I know him better than you do."

"You asked my advice."

"And you gave it to me." Leigh pulled at the collar of her blouse. "I think you're wrong."

"Fine." Shaking her hair free, Tracy began to brush it furiously.

"Would you like a bacon and tomato sandwich?" Leigh must have sensed she'd gone too far. Her voice had a small penitent sound.

"No thanks. I'll grab a hot dog in town."

"Tracy." Leigh grinned lopsidedly. "I'll take the shirts back."

"A wise decision."

THE OBEDIENCE CLASS had attracted many who had no dogs and only wanted to escape the confines of their homes for the comparative coolness of the park on this sultry June evening.

Onlookers sipped iced pop and spread blankets on the grass and visited with each other. The ice-cream truck, offering snow cones and Eskimo pies, was doing a booming business.

Ryle, wearing a tan shirt and white jeans, stood in the center of a circle made by his four-footed students and their handlers. Tracy sat some distance away, near the place she'd chosen to park. She couldn't hear very well, but at least she wouldn't be so easily spotted. By Ryle, who might have invented some new humiliation to get back at her for jilting him. Or by Willie, who was conditioned to think of food whenever he saw her and might decide to break the line up to come and beg.

Michael looked very adult in his summer plaid shirt and with his wet-combed hair, carefully parted.

Many of the faces around her were familiar—and many were actually smiling at her. She was greeted by old school chums and by old baby-sitting customers and her now grown charges. Some people spoke their welcomes with enthusiasm. Some looked forward to her opening; at least, they said they did.

She glanced at her watch. Michael and Willie had broken away from the others. They were running toward her at top speed. Ryle called his name, but Michael kept coming.

Super, she thought, as he skidded toward her. What now?

"He picks on me," the boy exploded, his face scarlet. "He says stuff to make people laugh at Willie, too."

"Are you sure?"

"I don't want my dog in his stupid old class. But I already gave him the eighteen dollars like you told me, Tracy. Ask for your money back."

The group was breaking up anyway. Or had Ryle called a stop early because of Michael? He started toward them with his head down and his purposeful showdown walk. Fortunately, a woman and her poodle intercepted him to ask a question.

"Let's go," Tracy said, springing up.

"Can't I ride home with Dave and his dad? They've got a pickup truck and we're gonna stop for pizza."

"Tomorrow's a school day."

"We'll be home by bedtime."

"Oh, all right." She dug into her pocket. "I think I have a dollar here and some change."

Michael handed her Willie's leash. "Dave's dad is gonna pay."

"No, Michael, wait."

"See you." He tore away, dodging as Ryle arrived and reached for him.

"Hold it, son. I want to talk to you."

"Somebody's waiting for me."

"Mike, come back here."

"I can't," he screeched and dashed off.

"Well-behaved kid you've got there," Ryle told her through tight lips.

Tracy squared her shoulders. If there was going to be a confrontation, it would concern the two of them—not her brother. "He's upset because you made fun of Willie."

"I did what?" He squinted, and hooked his thumbs in the pockets of his jeans.

"I'm sure you didn't do it intentionally. Willie is too old to be taking lessons."

"Willie wasn't the problem. Your brother wants to be praised constantly and assured that he has the best dog of the bunch."

"In other words, he's typical of most kids."

"Maybe. But most kids don't throw a temper tantrum if it doesn't happen."

The smile she gave him was at least as sincere as the one he offered. "As I've said, I'm sure Michael took your corrections too much to heart. He's sensitive."

"I can see that." Ryle snorted his disbelief.

"He's strong willed, I'll admit. And I'm glad. I want him to be able to bear up under the slings and arrows that are sure to be aimed at him in this life."

"There's nothing wrong with him that a half-dozen stinging swats where he sits down wouldn't fix."

"That's an old-fashioned prescription, doc." She released the dancing Willie into the car, slid behind the wheel and slammed the door harder than necessary, signaling that their discussion was finished.

Ryle rested a hand on the edge of the window frame and leaned toward her. "He's not the only one in the family who might benefit from the same treatment."

Planning to zip away and leave him standing at the curb, preferably off balance, she started the ignition and stepped on the accelerator. The engine began to turn over, then stopped. She tried again. Nothing. So much for her dramatic exit. She would have screamed if he hadn't been standing there.

"Move over. Let me give it a try."

"It'll start. It's just temperamental."

"That figures. Okay, Whelan. Whatever you want." He backed away a few steps, then wheeled suddenly around.

"Wait," she called, visions of herself being towed again overshadowing the remnants of her pride. "If it wouldn't be too much trouble . . ."

She slid out to let him in, not wanting to sit beside him. The derision in his eyes said that he'd tuned in on her reasons. After a few attempts, he pulled the hood latch and got out, too.

"Is it serious?"

If he answered, she didn't hear him. Someone was laughing loudly and theatrically. Tracy looked through the slowly dispersing crowd to see Suzanne, whose kelly-green dress caught her eye at once. Then she noticed the car. It was the black one she'd seen in the alley. The driver, the one who was joking with Suzanne, was the same boy. At least he wore a similar shirt and baseball cap. Could the girl have sweet-talked him into doing what he'd done to Tracy's shop the other day?

Tracy stared at them. Had he done the spray painting too? She remembered Leigh's certainty that Suzanne was somehow responsible—and she remembered laughing it off, arguing that Suzanne was far too fastidious to be sneaking around with a can of spray paint. But what if she'd persuaded this boy to do it instead? Maybe she'd even paid him. Tracy's mind was spinning with theories and suspicions. Had Leigh been right all along? But that still didn't explain why Suzanne—and that boy—would want to damage her shop. And her reputation.

"Ryle." Tracy touched his shoulder, forgetting for the moment their less-than-affectionate relationship.

The action surprised him and he struck his head on the raised hood. "Dammit!"

"Do you know that boy?" She couldn't keep the urgency from her voice.

His eyes followed her pointed finger. "Vince Dierker. He works at a 76 station on the highway. Why?"

"Do you know anything about him?"

"He has a pit bull who's overdue for shots. Why?"

"Just curiosity."

"Hi, you two." Suzanne had spotted them and hurried over.

"Hi," Tracy answered, beginning to feel foolish and a little ashamed. By assuming that Suzanne had influenced Vince into committing the vandalism, she was doing the same thing people had done to her ten years before, when Scott was taken into custody for starting the fires.

"Car trouble again?" Suzanne's lipstick was too dark. Her eyelids were adamantine blue. She looked older—more sophisticated. Her smile was a mask. "Why fuss around with this old heap? My father would buy you a shiny new one—like that." She snapped her fingers.

There was a look of such open animosity on Suzanne's face that Tracy was shocked. She glanced down at Ryle, but he obviously hadn't seen it. He was still tinkering with the engine and he seemed to be deliberately ignoring the girl.

"Ryle." Suzanne cooed his name and made circles on his back with the heel of one hand. "Did you know Tracy and I are related?"

"No, I didn't know that." He didn't look up.

"My daddy is her sugar daddy." Her giggle was malevolent. "Isn't that what you call men who pamper their pretty ladies with all kinds of presents? Anyway, you should see the expensive fixings he bought for her shop. Why wouldn't he buy her a car, as well?"

Ryle straightened up too quickly, hitting his head on the upraised hood again—harder this time. He glared at Tracy as if she'd struck the blow herself. "Do you have any rags?"

"In the trunk. I'll get them."

"It's so cute to see my uptight, upright father as moonstruck as a high school boy," Suzanne went on. "He's got it bad."

"That's enough." Tracy handed Ryle a rag to wipe the grease off his hands. "Your father bought me those chairs, yes. But we have an arrangement. I intend to pay him back."

"No one is doubting you will, dear. One way or another."

"Do you want to try the ignition again?" Ryle growled.

"Oh, by the way, before I forget . . ." Suzanne sidled between him and the car, slid her arms around his neck and kissed him on the mouth.

His color deepened, but otherwise he showed no reaction. "What was that for?"

"For being so sweet to me and letting me hide from Daddy," she said girlishly. When Ryle didn't respond, she added, "You know. The day he showed up at your office— with Tracy." He frowned but remained silent.

"May I have a ride home?" she wheedled. "My lift has disappeared."

"I suppose so. If we ever get this car out of here." He nodded in Tracy's direction. "How about trying the ignition again?"

"Can I have your car keys?" Suzanne's voice was small and pleading. "I'll meet you there. I have to speak to somebody first." She coyly laid a hand on his arm.

"Phony, two-faced, conniving little—" At Ryle's sharp glance, Tracy abruptly broke off her muttering. "Don't mind me. Just talking to myself again." She gave him a false, wide smile.

He turned back to Suzanne, his expression impassive once more. "You don't need the keys. The door's unlocked."

"Oh yes, I almost forgot. You don't believe in locks." She made a clicking sound with her tongue. "Honey child, you are too trusting."

"You may be right," he muttered under his breath.

"Doctor Tanner?" A gray-haired woman with a Pekingese cradled in her arms came toward him, fluttering her fingers. "Must I put a chain around my angel's neck? She's used to her own soft little collar. It's velvet."

"The choke chain won't hurt her, Mrs. Meek," he assured her. "It's part of her training."

"I don't like it." The woman thrust out her lower lip as though she were about to cry. "I'm not sure she'll forgive me."

Ryle patted her hand. "Muffin will know that you're doing it out of love."

The woman raised heavily crayoned eyebrows. "Do you think so?"

"I know so."

"I'm forever thanking you," Tracy said when they were alone and the engine started with the turn of her key.

"Forget it." The texture of his shirt was coarse. One edge of the collar had rubbed a reddish place on his neck. Did he do his own laundry? she wondered. His teeth were clamped together and he seemed to be holding back his temper with great effort.

It didn't matter that they were at outs with each other. Probably they always would be. Her memories of their times together were an almost physical ache, an ache that was growing in strength. An ache that might force her to hurl aside common sense and throw herself into his arms. She loved the shape of his mouth and the line of his jaw—even when he was judging her harshly, as he was judging her now.

His contempt should have been what she wanted. It would keep him clear of her—and keep her clear of temptation and the powerful aphrodisiac of his mere presence. Yet she couldn't bear to have him go on believing the lies she feared he believed. About her and Howard Barclay.

"I can't imagine what made Suzanne go on like that."

"I'm glad she did. It helped me understand a few things." There was perverse satisfaction in his tone. The girl's outburst had created an arena for his denouncement of her.

"You don't understand anything."

"What you do with your life is your affair. As long as I'm not caught in the middle again."

"It wasn't the way she made it sound!"

A muscle twitched at the corner of one eye. "It sounds to me as though history is repeating itself—in a new generation. Maybe you'll have more luck with the old man."

"All right, Tanner. You go ahead and believe what you want. You will anyway. I can't change that."

She didn't sigh or fasten him with a regretful look. Sighing and regrets could come later when she was alone, and she couldn't really blame him for feeling the way he did. Adjusting the seat cushion over the broken spring it covered, she raised her chin, pressed her foot on the accelerator and pulled away.

CHAPTER TEN

A SCHOOL PICNIC in Council Grove was an event that involved the entire community, rivaling the Fourth of July celebration that would take place in another two weeks. Red, white and blue banners were stretched across the main streets. Flags waved from windows and balloons were released in the town square. Merchants displayed signs for weeks in advance. They donated prizes, and some even closed their businesses early. A carnival on the fairgrounds a few miles out of town added to this year's fun—or chaos, depending upon one's point of view.

Several other schools from nearby towns had chosen the same date and site for their picnics, and Edmonton, their closest neighbor, would meet Council Grove at the end of the day for a softball game to decide the championship.

Leigh wasn't planning to attend the festivities. "Are you mad, girl? I have hundreds of things to do to get ready for the barn dance. If I could count on Ryle being there to hold my hand, I might be persuaded. But what with acting as a judge at the livestock show and then watching over the kids' craft booth, he'll be too busy to notice anyone."

Until the last minute Michael hadn't wanted to go, either. Picnics were for little kids. There were always flies on the food and the sun was too hot. Actually he was outraged that his craft project, a beaded belt, hadn't been accepted for the youth club display. But when he learned that Dave's father would be driving the van instead of Ryle, he changed his mind about going.

"Who cares if I'm not Doc Tanner's sissy favorite?" he asked as he departed.

The early-morning heat had warned of the sizzling afternoon that was now upon them.

"Did you do a head count, Miss Whelan?" The teacher's usually sleek French twist was tousled and the tail of her white blouse had slipped out of the waistband of her trim blue slacks. "All right, children." She clapped her hands when Tracy nodded. "Tigers to the left, with Miss Whelan. Leopards to the right."

The idea of giving each group of children the name of an animal to keep them together had been adopted enthusiastically by the adults. The children were less pleased. Most wanted to be lions and tigers. They balked at being classified as zebras or elephants. Some of the older ones referred to their rival groups as skunks and an overweight boy was pronounced a hippo.

"Lucky you." The teacher said to Tracy as she patted her damp forehead with a crumpled wad of Kleenex. "You've taken your group through the midway already. Now you can relax and look at the lovely things in the main tent. The ladies' quilts are breathtaking. And the needlepoint. Even the work the children have done. It's hard to believe these little ones would sit still long enough to tackle any project so time consuming. Ryle Tanner does have a way with youngsters, doesn't he?"

Yes, he knows how to crack the whip, Tracy thought ruefully. Which was why he resented Michael, who had a mind of his own. And why Michael resented him.

"I'd have stayed in that tent for hours," Mrs. Campbell went on, "just browsing. But the children want to go, go, go. And of course we adults must keep up with them or they make fun of us, don't they?" She sighed. "Especially when it comes to roller coasters and Whirly Wheels."

Tracy nodded her agreement. "They like nothing better than seeing a grown-up who's too 'chicken' to ride. Tell you what. I'll trade itineraries with you."

The woman blinked in disbelief. ''But the children still have eight ride tickets apiece to use. Could you bear to go through all that again? Not to mention the endless line-ups in the broiling sun.''

''I don't mind.'' Tracy did mind. The thought of boarding another twisting, turning, stomach-jolting car almost made her lose her breakfast. But the farther she kept from Ryle, the better. They'd be sure to come face-to-face in the main tent. Surrounded by Tigers, she'd have to comment appreciatively on the children's work. Which meant talking to Ryle. And talking to Ryle meant exchanging more verbal jabs.

''Quiet down, everyone.'' The teacher's voice was shrill. Undoubtedly she feared Tracy would come to her senses. ''There's been a change. Miss Whelan will take the Leopards. The Tigers will go with me. We'll meet back here at our picnic table in exactly two hours. Remember. Two hours. Section E. Table six.''

The decision to ride the Whirly Wheel was unanimous—if Tracy's vote wasn't counted. She sat between two fragile-looking little girls she thought might be frightened. But they giggled, while she gripped the bars until her knuckles turned white. They spilled out of the car eager for more, while she staggered, clutching her stomach.

The Grasshopper was next. Inoffensive enough to look at, it had cars in the shape of its namesake, with cute grasshopper faces. Looks were deceiving. When it went into action, a canvas top swooped down to trap its occupants, shutting off all light, and they were lurched, rocked, and twisted in the near darkness.

''Space Flight!'' one of the boys yelled next, speeding ahead and pointing. The other children seconded his suggestion. Tracy groaned. Still six more tickets left. The long, curving line would be a blessing this time. It would give her stomach a chance to settle.

''Whelan.''

Ryle? She turned to see him beckoning to her. He had two small girls in tow and wore a pained expression on his face. Her sacrifice had gone for nothing.

"I thought you'd be at the crafts booth," she said.

"Would that I were. I have an emergency here and I need your help."

"Oh?"

He went on to explain that a woman had left her purse somewhere and asked him to watch her girls while she ran back to look for it.

"I gotta go to the bathroom," one of the girls piped up. "I gotta go now!"

"Would you handle this?" he pleaded.

Tracy hesitated. "You'll have to take charge of my group while I'm gone."

"Fair enough."

"It means riding the Space Flight."

He twisted his face comically. "Understood."

"Hey, doc," one of the boys called, waving his arms. "We're gonna zoom through outer space."

Ryle hunched his shoulders. "I can hardly wait."

In the rest room, Tracy splashed cool water on her face, combed her hair hastily, and pinned it back with clips. Her nose was already sunburned. She'd forgotten her lip gloss, and somehow, she'd managed to get a smear of chocolate ice cream on her blouse. Scrubbing at it only made it worse.

"You're a mess," she advised her reflection.

"You're a sloppy eater, Miss Whelan," one of her charges told her.

"I resent that. I didn't even have any ice cream."

The girls' mother had returned with her purse by the time Tracy arrived. The Leopards had settled into their space cars and Ryle was folding his long legs into one himself.

"Hey, Miss Whelan," one of the children called, spotting her even though she had tried to merge with the crowd. "Hurry up. You can still make it. There's room."

"Uh—no thanks." She smiled sweetly and backed away. "That wouldn't be fair. I didn't stand in line."

"Go ahead." A man who'd been waiting just behind the Leopards made a gallant sweeping gesture for her to pass him.

"I couldn't. Really."

"Come on, girly," the ride man called.

"There's room with Doc Tanner," someone suggested. "He's got a car to himself."

Ryle slid back on the seat to make room for her to squeeze between his knees, and the seat belt was fastened around them both. The car nosed upward, jolted one position to allow the next couple to get on, and Tracy was slammed backward.

"I'm sorry."

"Do you hear me complaining?"

"Kiss her, doc!" The Leopard in the car just ahead of them snickered, turning around to ogle at them through his laced fingers. He made kissing sounds and the children in the next two cars joined in.

Another jolt and she was slammed against her riding partner again. "I'm sorry."

"Relax," Ryle told her. "I can take it."

Achingly conscious of his arms around her, she cleared her throat and reached out for the thread of impersonal conversation that would put distance between them—psychologically, if not physically. "Michael was disappointed when you didn't put his belt on display."

"To put it mildly. He ripped the thing to pieces and stomped on it."

"I thought it was beautifully done."

"You're his sister. You have to think that. It was sloppy work."

"He's only nine years old."

"Come by the booth and see some of the work turned out by nine-year-olds."

"People know the work is done by children. They don't expect perfection."

"There are projects for every level of skill. Mike could have chosen something simpler. He wanted to do the belt because he figured he'd get more points for it. Then he took shortcuts. Deliberately attached the beads at longer intervals so he'd get it done faster. The wallet was unacceptable. So was the belt."

"I didn't see the wallet."

"I know you didn't. He threw it away when I told him it would have to be done over."

The car lurched upward again. Then again. Ryle's arms went around her of necessity, steadying her, and she was helpless to avoid it. One more jolt and they were on their way.

As they climbed nearly straight up, she was aware only of the familiar warmth of his body, pressed beneath hers. Then they plunged and she forgot everything but the vertiginous sensation of falling. Up they climbed again, jerking backward and forward, until they reached the top. Then they relentlessly plunged again. Then up again and down. And again.

Oh, no, she thought, clutching at Ryle's arms. Don't let me get sick. Not now. Please.

She felt fifty years older when at last, mercifully, she could climb out, with Ryle's help.

"Exit to the left," the ride man recited in a bored-sounding voice.

"Let's get over in the shade," Ryle suggested, still supporting her as they walked. "Here's a bench. Now put your head lower than—Tracy!"

There was no time to explain. With a low moan, she made a dash for the rest room, clapping a hand over her mouth. For the moment, she didn't care about the hoots and cat-calls that followed her.

By the time she returned, the Leopards had been ushered onto another ride, with instructions to wait until Ryle came back for them or else. Knowing him, she had no doubt that they'd wait.

"I feel like such a fool," she said, fearing she might have to run for the ladies' room again without warning.

"If getting sick on a carnival ride makes you a fool, you're not alone. Don't worry about it. You made the kids' day."

"Super."

"How many rides was that for you anyway? What are you trying to do, break some kind of record?" When she gave him a puzzled glance, he lowered his head sheepishly, raked a hand through his hair and looked at her through a thick fringe of lashes. "Okay. So I watched you. To be honest, I came out on the midway for the express purpose of spying on you. You looked so damned cute trying to pretend you were enjoying yourself."

Nausea returned and she gripped the bench.

"Still feeling sick?"

She pressed a hand to her quivering middle. "I've had it for today. What am I going to do with my Leopards?"

"I know something that'll make a new woman of you."

"I should be so lucky."

"Wait here. Don't move." He dashed off and within minutes he was back holding a large pickle wrapped in wax paper. Breaking it in two, he held one half out to her. "This is a never-fail remedy. Take it."

She drew back. "What is it?"

"What does it look like? Suck on it. It'll settle your stomach."

"No thanks." She didn't want to seem ungrateful, but dill pickles didn't agree with her. They made her break out in a rash.

"Give it a try."

"No. I'll be okay. Maybe you should get the children."

Through clenched teeth, he said, "I'm not offering you a bloody town house or a Cadillac convertible. It's just a pickle. No strings attached. What's wrong? Afraid Barclay might stroll by and see us together?''

She stared down at her feet. Someone had dropped a snow cone. It was melting into a sticky puddle. Her stomach turned over.

"You read me wrong, Whelan," Ryle went on. "You're out of my life. The past is dead. The fact of that is clear in your every word, your every glance. You almost cringe whenever I touch you. I didn't mean anything personal here. I was only trying to help."

He went on about things she should have been relieved to hear. About how he wouldn't bother her again. And how they'd have to learn to live in the same town without feeling uncomfortable if they happened to run into each other.

"The first time you hurt me," he said, "and you *did* hurt me, we were kids. I can't hold you accountable. The second time, it was your fault. But if I ever let it happen again, I'd sure as hell deserve it."

"I don't know what to say."

"It's all been said." He stood up, looked at the dripping pieces of pickle, and let them drop into a nearby trash container. "I'll finish up the ride tickets with the kids and see they get back to Harriet Campbell. You stay put until you feel better."

"I can't let you do that."

His expression softened almost imperceptibly. "What are friends for?"

She didn't stay on the bench after he'd left. Wanting to be far away from the head-splitting raucousness of the midway, she walked toward the wooded area on the other side of the picnic grounds. It didn't soothe her as much as she'd hoped it would. The deep shade, the cooling overhead branches and the twittering bird talk couldn't help her escape the turmoil of her own regrets. The regret of knowing what might have been. Of knowing it was too late to unravel the tangled web of motives and feelings—hers and Leigh's and Ryle's. For a while, Tracy wandered aimlessly among the trees, trying to imagine what her life in Council Grove would be like from now on.

By the time she felt ready to join the others, the practice for the ball game had begun. The crowds waiting for rides had thinned considerably. People were finding seats in the bleachers.

While scanning the sea of faces, she found a familiar one. Vince Dierker was standing under the trees north of the ball field, watching. He wore the same baseball cap he'd been wearing when she chased him. She walked toward him.

"Vince, I'd like a few words with you," she began.

He leaned against a tree with a show of nonchalance and looked at her through half-closed eyes. "What about?"

"I think you already know." With a show of her own, one of calm assurance, she told him that she didn't plan to make trouble for him. She only wanted the vandalism to stop. If it continued she'd have no choice but to tell the sheriff who was responsible.

He lifted one shoulder. "I didn't do anything."

Tracy felt her anger rising as she spoke. "I think you did. You and your... friend. I think you know who I mean, Vince. Is she paying you?"

"Hey, you got no right to say that!"

Tracy looked hard at the boy. "Really? Isn't there something you ought to say?"

"I already told you. I didn't do anything!"

The discussion was getting loud and drawing an audience of its own. Nothing could be gained by continuing it. Tracy turned away.

"Maybe you should go back where you come from," Vince called quietly after her.

But not so quietly that Tracy didn't hear him. She whirled around, jabbing her finger in his direction. "This is where I come from, Vince. Understand? And this is where I'm staying."

CHAPTER ELEVEN

"MICHAEL, IS THAT YOU?" Tracy took her foot off the sewing machine pedal when the screen door slammed. Her only answer was a strangled sob, the thudding of footsteps and another door slamming—the door to her brother's room.

So much for getting her skirt hemmed before she went to the shop. It was the only thing she had to wear that would be halfway suitable for Leigh's shindig. The budget didn't allow for anything new, especially something that would be worn so seldom.

"Michael?" She knocked on the boy's door, then turned the knob and pushed, moving aside the hassock he'd put there to let her know that she wasn't welcome.

"I didn't say come in." He was sitting with his back against the wall, chin propped on his fists, elbows on his bent knees.

"What's wrong?"

"Everything. I hate this stupid town and all the stupid people in it."

Me, too, she almost blurted out, the child inside her wanting to sit against the wall beside him and weep over her own frustrations. "Would you like to ride into town with me?"

"Big deal."

"I have some things to take care of at the shop, but afterward we could stop for a hot dog and a shake."

"Dum-dum Tanner. He hates me and I'm glad. Because I hate him, too."

Now what was Ryle up to? Sliding the hassock closer to the side of her leg, she sat as near the boy as she dared. "What did he do, honey?"

"He kicked me out of his stupid club. He said I can't come back anymore." Tracy saw the shine of tears in her brother's eyes as he added, "Can't go on the overnighter, either."

She pressed her lips together hard, resisting the impulse to tousle his hair. That would only have made him react with even greater anger. She sensed he didn't really hate Ryle, in fact was probably a bit in awe of him. "Why would he do that?" she asked at last.

"Somebody broke one of the windows in his yucky house. He says I did it."

"Did you?" she asked gently.

Michael only glared at her.

"What made him think you did it?"

"He thinks I do everything, that's what. He always does. Some kid told him he saw me there. The liar. See, this kid doesn't like me, 'cause I beat him in the sack race. He said he'd get back at me."

"And Ryle took this other boy's word? Was that the only evidence he had?"

"He doesn't need evidence. He hates me. Right from the first day he picked on me."

Mr. Right and Wrong. Mr. Fair Play. Ryle was so caught up in his own image of himself, he might not even realize that he was acting like a dictator, flinging around accusations and "off-with-his-head" decrees.

Tracy's throat tightened and she held herself still as her spreading anger threatened to reveal itself to the already distraught child. In the blank whiteness of the ceiling, where she forced her attention, she saw the world as she had seen it a decade before. She'd been little more than a child at the time, yet people had pointed their self-righteous fingers at her and hadn't hesitated to pronounce her guilt.

"It's just a misunderstanding, honey," she finally managed to say. "We'll straighten it out."

A glimmer came into the boy's eyes. He knew her too well to accept the bland picture she tried to present. "Are you gonna tell him off, Trace? Can I come along?"

"It won't be anything like that," she assured him. "Ryle and I will discuss it, that's all."

"And you'll make him take me back?"

"I can reason with him, and if that doesn't work . . . well, I promise we'll do something that's just as much fun as his overnighter. Okay?"

Michael kicked at the edge of his dresser with one tennis shoe. "Like what?"

"I don't know." She leaned forward, catching him off guard, to press her lips against his damp forehead. "But for now, don't tell Leigh where I've gone."

"Yeah." He twisted his face into an expression of disgust. "She'd be on his side. He's her Prince Charming."

If the car had sprouted wings and flown, Tracy couldn't have driven to town fast enough to suit her. She kept hearing her mother's warning, the words echoing over and over in her mind. It was the day she'd given in and allowed Tracy to take Michael to Council Grove.

"You'll have to fight his battles for him, Tracy," her mother had cautioned. "Michael will be a stranger in a small town—and small-town people aren't the most tolerant in the world. They tend to run with the herd; you know that better than anyone. He'll feel like an outsider and he'll probably always be treated like one. I just want you to know the risks you're taking—for yourself and for him."

At the time, Tracy had considered her mother's warning rather melodramatic. It had more to do, she thought, with her family's sense of bitterness about the events that had forced them to leave Council Grove. But surely people wouldn't hold the tarnished reputation of one Whelan against another—a much younger one, at that. Would they? She was beginning to wonder.

There he was. She took the corner without braking just as Ryle came out of his office, and screeched to a halt at the curb in front of him.

"What the hell?"

"We have to talk," she said, glaring as she marched past him and went inside.

"I haven't got time for your nonsense, lady."

"You'll make time for this."

"I make time for medical emergencies. An animal in need of immediate attention. Otherwise—"

"You're completely despicable, Ryle. Your quarrel is with me. What kind of man are you to take it out on a little boy?"

He followed her inside and closed the door. "If you'd made a telephone call, you could have saved yourself a trip. Your brother is out. Period. No discussion."

"I didn't telephone because I wanted to see your face when I told you what I thought of you. And I wanted you to see mine when I assured you that you won't be allowed to torment Michael to satisfy your own vengeful nature. I'll fight you any way I can."

He set his medical bag on the counter and slapped a hand across its metal catch. "A fight is exactly what you're going to get if you ask me to allow your brother to flaunt all the rules and walk over everybody just because he's your brother."

"You're much harder on him than on the others—just because he's my brother. All I ask is that you treat him exactly the same as you'd treat anyone else."

"Are you?"

"You condemned him without proof. You took another boy's word over his."

"A boy who doesn't lie."

"And Michael does?"

"Yes."

"How dare you!"

"I dare because there isn't the slightest doubt that he broke that window. He was furious about the belt and the wallet, and God knows what else—it doesn't take much. Now, I'll have to find the time to buy new glass and replace the window—time I can't afford. In return, I told him that I expect him to weed the side yard. He refused."

"To do the weeding would have been to admit guilt."

"Right. And he'd be a better kid for it."

"What makes you a master of child psychology? What do you know about children?"

"I've dealt with them—a lot of them—for a lot of years."

"Only under optimum circumstances. Only for a few hours at a time—a few days at the most. When the going gets rough, you can send them home to their parents. You expect them to behave like miniature adults, complete with maturity and self-discipline."

"No, I don't. But I do expect honesty. And I expect them to understand the consequences of their actions. How else can they learn?"

"Maybe by example? If you showed them some tolerant and humane behavior, then they'd— On second thought, forget it! Tolerance and humanity from Ryle Tanner? Or from anyone else in this damned town? Not likely!"

He made an exaggerated display of checking his watch. "Now that you've had your tantrum, do you want to go? I'm running late." He dragged his bag off the counter and curled his fingers around the doorknob.

"Wait." She blew her hair out of her eyes. "I'll weed your damn garden."

"No way. Michael does it himself, or he's out of the club."

"You see?" she threw at him. "That proves it. Your sole purpose in setting that penalty is to bring my brother down."

"I don't make war on children."

"Not unless you have it in for their sister."

"This isn't getting us anywhere." He set the bag down again with an air of resignation, snatched up the phone and jabbed the buttons. "Mac? Ryle Tanner. Something's come up. Would tomorrow morning be okay. You sure? Thanks. I'll be there."

"You didn't have to do that."

"Yes, I did." His voice was dangerously quiet. He brushed past Tracy to snap the lock on the door, moving on silent, agile feet. Then he turned back to her. "Looks like there's only one way to talk to you, Whelan. It seems the only time we can be civil to each other is when you're in my arms."

His reference to their previous intimacy was jarring and unfair. Her fingers curved around the top button of her blouse in a defensive gesture. She'd left home in such haste she hadn't changed into her demure, on-the-job costume. The fit of her blouse was too snug, leaving occasional gaps that showed glimpses of her plain white sport bra.

"That doesn't say much for our relationship," she said.

"You made it clear what that relationship was." His eyes were unnaturally dark, darker than she'd ever seen them. His fists were clenched at his sides.

"You said you were in a rush," she said nervously.

"Not anymore." He wet his lips with his tongue, making her feel as though he were wetting hers. "My time is yours."

"Just like that." She snapped her fingers, but her hands were damp and the action made no sound.

He snapped his—with greater success. "Just like that."

"You may be able to cancel your appointments and rearrange your obligations with a single phone call. I can't. Anyway, I've said everything I've come here to say. I'm leaving. Open the door, please."

"Oh, no you don't, Whelan. We have unfinished business, you and I."

He caught her shoulders and they grappled soundlessly as he walked her backward, kicking aside the magazine table to shove her onto the reception couch. When she bounced up as if on springs, he shoved her down again, this time weighting her heavily into the cushions with his own body.

"Damn," he growled in mock frustration as in shifting over her, one of his long legs struck a lamp and toppled it. "I know I should have ordered a bigger sofa for this room."

"Yes," she hissed. "If you planned to use it to force yourself on unwilling women."

"Where is this unwilling woman? You want this as much as I do. Isn't it what you came here for? Isn't it?"

"That's not true," she shrieked. Wrestling him with new strength, she arched her back, rising and falling again, until he took her wrists easily in one hand and dragged them to a position above her head.

She lay back against the couch, her chest heaving, her breath quick and shallow—and not just from the exertion of struggling. She closed her eyes, feeling anger die away, feeling desire spring to full and raging life within her. Only Ryle had ever evoked a need this strong, this overwhelming. Only Ryle. She reveled in the intensity and the anticipation—and pushed away the dim knowledge that later she would reproach herself for her surrender.

He dipped his head to brush his mouth back and forth across her lips. "Too bad these have to be used for talking. If you could reserve them for kissing me, it would be perfect. God, I've missed the feel of you, the smell of you. The sweet taste of your mouth."

"It won't be any good like this, Ryle." Her plea came without force. She wanted him desperately.

"I'll chance it," he countered.

He released her hands and they fluttered helplessly to his back, to enjoy the wonderfully knit muscles she remembered.

"Aren't you going to tell me you love me?" he asked. "Like you did before?"

Her eyes flew open. "I was wrong to say it."

"That's true. We both know what it is you love."

His mouth was hard as he brought it down on hers. She felt his hands, ungentle in their urgency, rove the length of her back, the rounded line of her hip. She felt his body thrust against hers with a force, an excitement, that made her gasp and the small breathless sound was absorbed by their kiss. The taste of him filled her mouth. The scent of him filled her nostrils, the familiar clean scent of soap, heightened now by something else. By sweat. By lust.

Then he suddenly drew back. He caught her chin in one fierce hand and for a long moment looked deeply into her eyes. "It was almost worth it for this. All the torment you've put me through."

He caressed her ear with heated breath and outlined it wetly with the tip of his tongue. Her mouth, unready before, was ready now. She closed her eyes and waited. Nothing happened.

His weight shifted off her body. Her lips, unappeased, were raw and aching. Ryle stood on unsteady legs, adjusted his belt and began tucking his shirt more smoothly into his jeans.

"I said almost. But not quite. I have to agree with you, Whelan. This isn't the place or the time for passion. Go home." He drove his hands through his hair, slicking it back for only seconds before it fell forward again, framing the rocklike contours of his face.

It would have been kinder if he'd turned away, if he'd gone into the other room, or pretended to be occupied at his desk.

He offered no such kindness. Tall and watchful, he stood without saying anything, as one of his Blackfoot ancestors might have stood, supervising the eviction of a vanquished enemy whose life had been spared but whose lands were forfeit.

Tracy buttoned her blouse where it had come undone and smoothed her skirt with unsure hands, waiting for the tempest inside her to subside. She worked at the tangle of her hair with a pitiless comb and applied lipstick to her lips, though they were now chafed and needed no color.

It made her think of other times, painfully long ago, when he'd come early to watch her as she readied herself for their dates. She remembered how attentively he would gaze at her as she performed these same rituals, and how womanly she would feel, how confident and secure in his approval. But now, all she felt was shame.

"Tracy." His voice sliced neatly through the humid silence. "Don't ever come to see me again without Willie in your arms and needing attention, or you'll know what to expect." Lemony sunlight, filtered through the closed blinds, speckled his face and arms, making the episode between them seem nightmarish. "Let this be fair warning."

"Thank you," she said, in a crisp voice that wasn't her own.

"Thank nothing of it," he answered.

CHAPTER TWELVE

HELPING ED COLLINS staple crepe paper in place and hang Japanese lanterns had taken most of the day and hadn't done much to relieve Tracy's depression. He and two part-time workers had cleaned the grounds earlier. Everything looked festive and beautiful. Everything and everybody seemed to be under control—except Leigh, who was walking two feet above the ground.

Clearly as uncomfortable with their assigned decorating chore as Tracy was, the only time Ed said anything was when he hit his thumb with a hammer. Then at least he had the good grace to say it under his breath. Wearing his usual faded denim shirt and low-slung jeans, he went about his work as if he were driven, worry or anger, or both, making a deep furrow between his dark shaggy brows.

She couldn't stand it any longer. "You seem angry with me, Ed. Do you mind if I ask why?"

"You can ask."

"But will you answer?"

He let the staple gun swing downward and took the weight of it on his index finger. "Everything has changed since you got here."

"Changed in what way?"

She could have counted to twenty while he deliberated. And then the words tumbled out, rapid-fire.

"It's Leigh. She's changed. She used to come to me when she had problems. Used to ask me for advice about all kinds of things—the bills, the stables, the horses. Business stuff. When she was upset with that guy, that lawyer—she used to talk to me about it sometimes. Now she's got you. When she felt bad, I used to try and get her to feel better. Try and make her laugh. Usually it worked. We'd both end up laughing. Then she'd feel better and so would I." He swung the staple gun into position and reached for the last package of red crepe paper. "She doesn't do much laughing anymore. At least, not with me."

So that was it. Tracy might have guessed if she hadn't been so entangled with her own worries. Ed was in love with Leigh. That was why he'd stayed on and why he'd bought into the stables.

"It's important that we be friends, you and I," she said gently. "We both care for Leigh and want her to be happy."

He shook his head. "You're going to hurt her."

"I promise I won't."

"This business with Doc Tanner. You lead her on. Give her ideas. Make her think something's going to happen, when you know damn well it can't."

"How do you know it can't?"

Up until now, he'd kept his eyes averted or trained on the fence rail that he was carefully decorating with crepe paper. Now they struck hers with the full force of his accusation. "I suppose you've forgotten I was witness to a few things. Things that made it pretty damn clear. You and Doc Tanner."

Tracy's face warmed. "It isn't what you think," she protested. "Ryle and I knew each other years ago."

"We're not talking old times here, Miz Whelan. We're talking now." He laid down the staple gun and leaned back against the fence, staring at the scuffed toes of his boots. "Look," he said suddenly. "I'll say my piece this once. You might as well know. I've been hoping—someday—Leigh and I could become...real partners. Not just business partners. I mean, get married. I haven't asked her yet. I've been afraid to, now she's set her cap for Doc Tanner. And you've encouraged her," he insisted, ignoring Tracy's stuttering protests. "Leigh and I could have a real good marriage. We get along, always have. She needs me. And there's nothing I wouldn't do for her. Nothing. You remember that, Miz Whelan. I'm the one who loves her. Doc Tanner's a good man. He wouldn't hurt her, not on purpose. But she's going to get hurt all the same. And it'll be your fault. But *I'll* still be here. I'll pick up the pieces. Make her laugh again."

Whew, Tracy thought, still stunned by his words, that's more than he's said to me the entire time I've been here. She took a deep breath and tentatively lay a hand on his arm. "Thank you for telling me, Ed. I wish I'd..." They both heard Leigh's voice, overloud with excitement. Tracy stepped back and announced brightly, "We've done a great job as exterior decorators, I'd say. A terrific job."

Ed unexpectedly gave her a quick, shy grin. "Yup. Looks fit and proper for a shindig." He straightened and pushed himself away from the fence with both hands. "Well, I'd better head home and get myself ready."

"You *are* coming back?"

He looked over his shoulder at Leigh, who was supervising the placement of a large trestle table. "Do I have any choice?"

"I guess not," she said softly.

He smiled at her a second time, just the trace of a smile, before loping off. Now Tracy knew why he'd resented her. And she really couldn't blame him. They'd reached some understanding and it made things better, but it also made them worse. She wondered whether Leigh suspected how Ed felt and whether she could ever return his feelings. Chances were, she thought sadly, they'd all be hurt. Leigh and now Ed. Ryle. And her. She slowly gathered up fallen scraps of crepe paper, put them in the trash and set the mason jar of tacks in the utility cabinet next to the back porch.

Leigh met her at the door. "Why don't you take the first bath?" she asked.

"That's all right. You go ahead." Tracy headed for the refrigerator and the ice water.

"Nope." Leigh sidestepped into her path. Her eyes were round and tense. "The bathroom's all yours. I'll get dressed while you're in the tub. When you're done, come to my room, okay?"

Something was definitely brewing under Leigh's headful of pink plastic rollers. "What's up?" Tracy asked.

"Up? Nothing. Just put on your robe and mosey over there."

After a quick cool bath, Tracy hurried to Leigh's room— and came to an abrupt standstill in the doorway. A turquoise prairie dress lay across the bed, spread lovingly to show its three-tiered skirt to the most beautiful advantage. It had a nipped-in waist, a plunging neckline and was trimmed with silver rickrack. A three-by-five card with a happy face sticker was tucked under its silver belt. To Tracy, it read, For being my friend.

Tracy planted a fist on each hipbone in an attitude of determination. "Take it back."

"It called your name from the shop window. It's you."

"Tomorrow it can call someone else. It goes back."

"It's rude to refuse a thank-you present."

Outside the music had started. The band was warming up. Each of the instruments seemed to be playing a different tune. A car door slammed.

"Why on earth should *you* be thanking *me*? You found the shop for me. You made all the arrangements. Now you're letting Michael and me stay with you rent free. If anyone should be buying gifts, it's me."

"Speaking of buying things, you should see the dress I got myself," Leigh crooned, hugging herself the way she'd always done when she was excited as a child. Obviously she hadn't heard a word.

"Keep the tags," Tracy insisted. "I won't wear it."

"I've already tossed them out. The skirt you were planning to wear was only fit for the hobos' ball. You cut my hair for me, didn't you? And set it?"

"How many cuts and sets could you get for what that dress cost?"

"Oh, Trace, don't spoil the most wonderful night of my life. Please don't." When Tracy turned her back in exasperation, Leigh just came around to stand in front of her. "When people care about each other, it pleases them to give presents," she said earnestly. "Which is why I bought Ryle the shirt."

"Which you took back."

Leigh caught her lower lip between her teeth. "Which I gave to him. And it worked. He wasn't going to come. Now he said he'd stop in. I didn't have the nerve to ask him to be my date, but what the heck? I'm here and he'll be here. That's good enough for now."

"Oh, Leigh!"

"You like the dress?"

Tracy sighed. "I like it. How could I not like it?"

"You'll keep it?"

"I'll keep it. But we'll work out who pays for it later." She shook her head. If people kept making purchases for her, she'd never get out of debt.

Leigh's dress was designed to look like separates. The yellow peasant-style bodice was intricately embroidered with green thread. The long, swirling skirt was yellow too, with a green print that was stamped on but looked embroidered. She looked prettier than Tracy had ever seen her before. The darker, more carefully applied eye makeup brought her eyes out dramatically. The shorter, fuller hairstyle smoothed the squarish angles of her face. Ryle couldn't help but do a double-take when he saw her. Maybe he'd even be smitten.

She hugged Tracy three times and had to be pried away from the full-length mirror.

"Your public awaits, Cinderella," Tracy reminded her as strains of "Tennessee Waltz" filled the room.

"I have it all worked out. When Ryle arrives, I signal for a ladies' choice. I make sure I'm close to him, you see, and then I grab him. And—to add whipped cream to the cake—

the ladies' choice I've asked them to play is one that ends with the lady bestowing a kiss. Have I got guts or have I got guts?''

"You've got guts," Tracy agreed with a small laugh.

"By the way, Trace, you look almost as gorgeous as I do. Wear the silver and turquoise earrings I put on your dresser. They'll be perfect with that dress. You'll never guess where I got them. From Ed. He gave them to me last Christmas. And I didn't get him anything! But I'm sure he wouldn't mind if I lent them to you, just for tonight.''

Tracy adjusted the neckline of her dress to lie more symmetrically over the shoulders. "Thanks, but no. I'm not going to wear earrings.''

"You know what they say about baubles, bangles and beads and how they charm the adult male.''

"I'm not out to charm anyone.''

Leigh lingered in the doorway, her fingernails tracing the line of the plastic switch plate. "Ah, Trace, is it true what they're saying about you and Howard Barclay?''

"If you've heard that he claims to be sorry for the past and that he's kind enough to want to help me, yes, it's true.''

"Don't get so huffy. He might be a little old for you. But a girl could do worse.''

Tracy curled her hands into fists. "I'm trying not to strangle you, Ms Monahan, on your night to end all nights. But you of all people should know better than to listen to that kind of gossip—especially considering its source.''

"Okay, say no more. I only wanted to be sure.''

"Why?''

"Are you gonna come out here soon, Leigh? People are asking for you.'' Ed Collins was at the window, shading his eyes to peer through the screen. He was scrubbed and combed and he wore a brand-new blue Western shirt. It was a size too large and it looked suspiciously like one of the two shirts Leigh had shown her earlier. The shirts she'd bought for Ryle.

"I'll be there in a minute," Leigh said. "Go ahead. I'll meet you outside." She waited for him to leave. "Um, Trace, I was wondering. Would you do me a favor? Dance with Ed? I don't want him feeling left out. Most people make him feel uncomfortable, but I noticed he was getting along real well with you this afternoon."

"Why don't you dance with him? And where's Michael?"

"How can I dance with him? I have Ryle. Michael's out there guzzling punch—the nonalcoholic kind, I hope."

"Leigh?" Ed was back at the window sounding impatient. "Are you coming?" Leigh gathered her skirts and dashed for the door.

She couldn't have picked a better night for the dance if she'd ordered it from a catalog. The moon was close and every star in the heavens was out for the occasion. After expressing her regrets to Willie that a dog just didn't have a place at a people party, Tracy gave him a quick hug and went outside. She decided to make her entrance slowly, not wanting to be noticed. She would join the festivities only long enough to satisfy Leigh and to greet everyone who should be greeted. Then she would retire to her room and read, if she could concentrate with the sawing of the fiddles.

So she hung back, hovering in the shadows of the house, carefully watching the dancers. There was a sense of hectic gaiety, of excitement, heightened by all the colorful costumes. Most of the men had cooperated by wearing plaid shirts and cowboy boots. The women wore square-dance costumes of every imaginable hue. Still, Suzanne managed to stand out in a white dress trimmed in red. A line of red velvet bows had been fastened in her shining cluster of ebony curls and she wore an attached hairpiece to give the suggestion of longer tresses. She looked very beautiful and much older than her nineteen years. She stared right through Tracy, pretending not to see her.

A young man she'd never met before grabbed Tracy for "Dill Pickle Rag," then a man she should have remembered from high school—but didn't—whirled her around the floor, double time, to "The Girl I Left Behind Me," all the while rattling on about Scott's long-ago races with the highway patrol and the times Tracy had supposedly played Bonnie to his Clyde. Two more lively reels with semistrangers and she was winded. She had to take a rain check on the next dance and made her way to the refreshment table for a cold drink.

"Ladies' Choice," the fiddler called. "Come on, girls. Now don't be shy. Here's your chance to snag that guy."

Right on cue. Ryle was near the platform, though she hadn't seen him come in. He looked self-conscious in his fancy rust-and-yellow Western shirt—like a little boy dressed up against his will to attend a birthday party for someone he hardly knew.

Leigh was ready to make her move, but it was too late. Suzanne was closer and slid into Ryle's arms with the ease of a practised seductress. Even from where she stood, Tracy could feel the intensity of Leigh's fury.

She waited helplessly for the music to end. It seemed to go on and on, sounding muffled and faraway. She was watching Leigh, who hadn't moved since the dance began. Then, finally, the music slowed. The kiss was called and Suzanne took full advantage of it, settling her mouth firmly on Ryle's. Leigh flounced away, her wide skirt a flash of color. Tracy followed as quickly as she could, threading her way through the laughing couples.

Leigh wasn't at the refreshment table—though Michael was there, stuffing himself with cakes and fancy cookies. Tracy couldn't find Leigh behind the musician's platform, either. And she wasn't in the barn or the house. Where then? A flurry of small lies and platitudes, anything to soften her friend's disappointment, took shape in Tracy's mind as she stood at the edge of the dancing area again, rising on tiptoe to scan the crowd, a face at a time.

Her search was interrupted by Howard Barclay. "I've been looking for you," he said, and she noticed that his only concession to the informality of the occasion was the absence of a tie.

"Do you want to dance?" he asked. "I'd like to talk to you and this is the least conspicuous way."

She reluctantly agreed, more out of respect for their fledgling friendship, if she could call it that, than out of any desire to dance.

"I won't keep you long," he promised her. "I know there's talk going around about us and I'm sorry. It must be embarrassing."

"It doesn't matter." Tracy accepted his arm and allowed him to lead her into the bright circle of dancers. "If people can't find anything to gossip about, they'll invent it."

"True." He danced with smooth precision, as she'd suspected he would, guiding her through a series of intricate steps he executed without apparent thought. "I wanted you to know that Mr. Dierker came to see me this morning. Vince's father. He told me about his son vandalizing your shop. Unfortunately, it just confirmed what I already suspected. According to Vince, Suzanne goaded him into it. More or less blackmailed him, he claims, over some minor indiscretion or other. I have reason to believe he's telling the truth."

Tracy only nodded, unsure of what to say.

"I'm deeply sorry, Tracy. Sorry and ashamed." His voice was so low she had to strain to hear him. "It's why I bought the chairs. To make up for what she did to you. What we all did—Scotty, me. Now Suzanne...damaging your shop, starting those rumors." He fell silent for several minutes and Tracy stared down at her feet, concentrating on the dance steps, feeling pity and sadness well up in her.

She looked up, startled, as Howard cleared his throat. "There's something else I came to say. Suzanne will be leaving Council Grove; I've arranged for her to go east and live with her mother. Suzanne is...troubled. She needs help, professional help, and she can't get it here. I don't know what's gone wrong or who's to blame. But I do know things will only go worse with Suzanne unless she gets away from this town. Away from me.''

Tracy knew it was a painful admission for him to make. Clumsily, consolingly, she patted his arm, still unable to speak.

"I'll be going now." He smiled thinly. "I hope you won't think too badly of me, even if I deserve it.''

Before she could frame a protest, a denial, he was gone. She stood quite still for a moment, suddenly and dizzily aware of the music and the whirling dancers all around her. It took her a moment to get her bearings. She remembered that she had to search for Leigh, but just then one of the fiddlers called a change of partners and Tracy found herself in the arms of Ed Collins. He grinned at her shyly but seemed distracted. Trying to spot Leigh among the dancers, Tracy supposed.

Another change and she got a man she'd danced with earlier, the man who had reminisced about her and Scott.

Would the music never stop? she wondered, as she was obliged to take another partner and another. If the medley continued, inevitably she would get Ryle. The thought made her feel giddy. The room became a blur of color and a jangle of sound. It occurred to her that if she were to faint, she'd have to be carried out. She could use her indisposition as an excuse to leave the festivities, as ladies of another era had used their "vapors." It didn't happen. The baker, whose shop was down the street from her own and who was a rotund tribute to his own skills, spun her around three times, executed his low bow and turned her over to Ryle.

She was almost glad. The nightmare had become a reality—but a reality in which there was no nightmare. She was at home in his embrace. Even his simmering resentment couldn't change that, couldn't change the way she felt. The lights dimmed and the music grew slow and sweet, as if the musicians knew and were cooperatively providing an accompaniment suitable to the tenderness she harbored for this man who held her.

"I didn't expect you to be here." Her voice came out breathy and small instead of friendly and festive.

"I can't flatter myself that you made yourself beautiful for me then, can I?"

Was he saying, in his backhanded way, that she looked beautiful? She felt giddy again. A bit of banter was called for to save her from the quicksand of her treacherous emotions. "You look spiffy in that shirt."

Her attempt wasn't appreciated. He colored and his thumb pressed her wrist tentatively. "It seemed important to Leigh that I be here."

"She hoped the whole town would turn out."

"I think they did."

"She has a new hairdo."

"Your work?"

She nodded. "Did you tell her she looked pretty?"

He frowned down at her. "I told her she looked nice."

"Women like to be told they're pretty."

"You're going to lecture me on semantics?"

"No. There's a wide world of difference between the two words, though."

"Okay. I'll tell her before I go. Let up, okay? I've had one devil of a day."

"What happened?"

"It's not your problem."

"I suppose it isn't. I thought—"

"Oh, just drop it, would you?"

"Can we call a truce?" she asked, figuring it was worth a try. "It's too lovely a night to be snarling at each other."

"I don't put much faith in truce talks."

"That's the Blackfoot in you," she said solemnly.

"Maybe." A corner of his mouth quivered. "What terms did you have in mind?"

As she considered his question, she suddenly caught sight of Leigh, standing at the edge of the circle. Even in the muted light, she could see the coppery hair, the green-and-yellow dress. Where have you been, Tracy wanted to shout over the music and the laughter. I was worried sick! Several couples danced slowly by, obscuring her view. Then she saw Leigh again and for the first time she noticed who was standing with her. A girl in a white dress with red trim. Suzanne. And Leigh's head was bent, listening.

What could Suzanne possibly have to say to Leigh? It could only be lies. Unless...Suzanne knew about Tracy and Ryle—and she knew that Leigh was in love with him, too. Tracy went cold with anxiety. She lost awareness of everything except her fears for Leigh, her fears of what Suzanne might be saying. She tried to force Ryle to move closer to the edge of the dance area. Perhaps she could interrupt Suzanne before it was too late, she thought frantically, or at least overhear the conversation. Her movements were obviously confusing Ryle and he stumbled. They collided with another couple and his foot came down on the woman's instep.

"I'm sorry," Ryle said, reaching out to her. "Are you okay?"

The woman offered a brave smile as she hobbled off to the sidelines, supported by her dancing partner and trailed by Ryle and Tracy.

"Still trying to lead?" Ryle hissed in a furious undertone when he turned his attention to Tracy again.

"Why not?" she answered, hoping to make light of it. "It's a changing world."

As she spoke, she craned her neck, searching for Leigh, peering through the groups of brightly dressed dancers. She didn't see her. But she did see Howard. He was standing at the opposite edge of the dance floor, talking urgently to Suzanne. He was grasping her elbow as though he wanted her to come with him and she was shaking her head wildly.

Tracy watched them, puzzled. Where was Leigh? Howard looked up and noticed her. He smiled and shrugged, releasing Suzanne's arm. Then he raised his hand to Tracy in a signal of farewell.

Ryle didn't miss the gesture. His irises looked large and round and almost black. "Barclay seems to be leaving," he muttered with heavy sarcasm. "Maybe you should run over to him, get him to stay and dance with you again. Too late. Oh, well, better luck next time."

"Hi, you two." Suzanne minced toward them wearing a Cheshire cat grin. "Why don't you go dance with Leigh?" she suggested to Ryle. "I'd like to have a little girl talk with Tracy."

His eyebrows peaked. "What's all this about Leigh?"

"You poor innocent." Suzanne made a clicking sound with her tongue and gave his cheek a pat. "You missed the whole point of this barn dance, didn't you?"

"What did you want to talk about?" Tracy broke in quickly before the girl could say more.

"Can't we get away from all this noise?" Suzanne took the lead, walking with easy strides and swinging her arms as if she were as carefree as a child. The model's mincing walk had been abandoned temporarily in favor of whatever new role she'd chosen to play.

She moved purposefully toward the house and pushed open the kitchen door as casually as if it had been her own home. She sauntered into the half-lit room, propping herself against the counter. Tracy rather doubted that Suzanne's intention in singling her out was to say a fond goodbye or to apologize for the trouble she'd caused.

"What did you want to talk to me about?" she asked abruptly.

"I saw you with Father."

"And?"

"And I wanted to warn you that you're going to regret what you've done to me. He's sending me away because of you."

"No, Suzanne. Not because of me. Because of you. You've done this to yourself. You'll have to pay the price."

"Well, I've seen to it that you'll pay, too. And you'll wish *you* were the one leaving town."

Now the band was playing "The Varsuvianna." It was a number Leigh had especially wanted to dance with Ryle. Tracy knew the sensible thing would be to walk away from Suzanne, but she couldn't deny her curiosity. "Why do you dislike me so much?" she asked.

"Dislike isn't a word I would use." Suzanne tapped a finger against her lips and considered the question. "Despise would be more like it. I despise you because of what you did to Scotty. You destroyed him."

Avenging younger sister—was this the role she'd chosen, then? But the words lacked conviction. "I don't believe you loved your brother at all," Tracy said slowly, her idea only beginning to take shape. "You were jealous of him. Maybe you even hated him. Now you hate me because your father has turned to me in his unhappiness, trying to salvage something of the past. He's made mistakes—we all have. But it's not too late, you know. Maybe if you'd use all the energy you're wasting on hatred and self-pity to show him how—"

"Don't lecture me," Suzanne interrupted in a voice so laden with venom it quivered. "You have no idea how hard I've tried. From nursery school when I brought home pictures I'd drawn, to junior high when I nearly broke my neck trying to win awards for scholastic achievement. Scotty did nothing but bring disgrace on the family. But he was everything. I only attracted my father's attention when—" Her voice broke off when she realized she was losing control of herself and the situation.

"My reasons for despising you don't matter. Ryle will be the key. I've talked to Leigh. I've told her what I know about you two. Oh, she didn't believe me at first—her good friend Tracy wouldn't do that to her. But give her time to think about it. By tomorrow she won't want to be under the same roof with you. She'll force you out of town, and then—"

"That's enough." Tracy's mouth felt dry. She ran from the kitchen, letting the back door slap shut behind her, hearing Suzanne's high-pitched laughter following her out.

Where would Leigh have gone now? she thought despairingly. Where would Leigh go if she were feeling unhappy, angry, betrayed... The stables. Of course.

She ran through the yard, straight through a circle of square dancers, and shouldered her way past the small groups of revelers standing on the sidelines. She ran past Michael and another boy, pausing only long enough to give them a breathless warning to stay out of trouble.

She moved through the open stable door and came to a sudden stop, trying to quiet her breath, trying to listen for Leigh. Away from the festivities and screened from the night by three walls, the air was thick. It smelled of leather and burlap. It was thick with something else, too. Leigh's misery. Tracy leaned against a stall, feeling Roxy's warm breath in her hair, and waited. She could hear Leigh's desolate small sobs, her gulping attempts to swallow the tears. For what seemed a long time Tracy just waited, not even trying to form the words she would say to her friend.

A shadow swayed then, and Leigh came out of the tack room. Even in the half-light Tracy could see that her face was swollen and ravaged with weeping. "Is it true?" Leigh whispered hoarsely. "Is it true that Ryle kissed you—more than once?"

Tracy hesitated a moment too long.

"It's true, isn't it? What she said. Trace?" Leigh's eyebrows drew together.

"Leigh, I—" Tracy began.

"She told me you and Ryle spent the night together."

"You know we did. There was a storm. I couldn't get home."

"She said it was more than that. She said you—"

"That's a lie," Tracy cried. "It wasn't like that. We didn't—"

"She said you and he were...you know...at his office...and *here*..."

"Oh, Leigh, please, let me try and explain. I..."

Leigh's mouth opened but emitted no sound. She stared, wild-eyed, as though looking at something too horrible to comprehend. Tracy cautiously placed a hand on her friend's arm, but Leigh shook it off. "You're admitting that it's true, then," she said flatly.

"We went out to dinner together the night you took Michael to Moberly," Tracy started, praying she could make her friend understand. "You hadn't told me then that it was Ryle you cared about. We talked about old times and—"

"Why couldn't you have had the decency to tell me?" Leigh sobbed. "Why did you allow me to make a fool out of myself? It's the foulest, meanest, dirtiest trick anyone has ever played on me."

"I should have told you the first day. I realize that now."

"Yes. Now that you've been caught. Did you and Ryle have fun laughing at my pathetic attempts to look beautiful for him?"

"You know we didn't. Ryle doesn't know anything about it. As soon as you told me how you felt, I didn't go out with him again."

"Oh? Then Suzanne lied about everything? He never kissed you here, in my house?"

"Yes. But I didn't mean for it to happen."

"Were you trying to prove that you could take him away from me? That you could have any man you wanted?"

"No." Tracy hardly dared to breathe as the truth struggled to be free. "I love him, Leigh."

"You love him." Leigh's voice was a monotone.

Roxy whinnied and made thumping sounds against the sides of her stall. One of the other horses answered her. Leigh was past hearing anything. With dragging steps she made her way to the door. Her flared skirt caught on a nail that protruded from one of the four-by-four support posts and in trying to free it with trembling fingers, she ripped a long gash in the fabric.

A full minute seemed to pass as she looked at it blankly. With a strangled cry, she twisted her hands in the tear and ripped the skirt from waistband to hemline. Then she was gone.

CHAPTER THIRTEEN

THE INCH-WIDE GAP in the curtains showed that the sky was pale yellow. It was morning. Tracy sat on the edge of Michael's bed and smoothed a hand across his forehead. He turned over, settling with his back to her.

"Wake up. I have super news."

"What?"

"When I'm sure you're awake, I'll tell you." The extra time would allow her to don a proper air of enthusiasm.

"Is it about the overnighter? Did Doc Tanner change his mind?" He ground a fist into one eye and yawned.

"Better than that. I decided you were right. This town is stuck somewhere in the last century. Their softball team wasn't even able to win against a little one-horse place like Edmonton. We don't belong here. Now that school's out, we don't have to stick around. We're going home."

She waited for the whoop of joy. It didn't come. There wasn't even a half-hearted "neat-o!" Wide awake now, Michael sat up. His chest and shoulders were bare. He'd been sleeping in his underwear again. "How can we leave?"

"I thought about it all last night. I'm going to go see Howard Barclay. Maybe he can help me figure a way to get out from under. I know I'll probably lose a lot of the money I've invested already, but . . ." She swallowed and drew a deep, slow breath. Why was she prattling on to a nine-year-old about her financial problems? Didn't he have enough to contend with just having a harebrained sister? "That's life, m'lad. You win some and you lose some. We'll be back in

Kansas City in time for you to go on that YMCA trip to Lake of the Ozarks."

"Who cares about some dumb old lake?" Michael bunched the quilt up and hugged it to his chest. "I've been there a million times."

"Not quite."

"I don't want to go."

"You hate it here."

"I don't, either. I hate it there."

She pressed a finger to her lips, warning him to keep his voice down. She didn't want to wake Leigh. "We'll get a really nice apartment. Maybe I can even swing one with a pool."

"There's a pool here. At Garfield Park. And Leigh's gonna give me my own pony."

"I don't think so, baby."

"I'm not a baby and I'm not going to move again." He flipped onto his stomach and pulled the covers over his head, so that only his bare legs stuck out. "You go back if you want. I'm staying here."

Tracy realized she should have guessed that this would be Michael's reaction. When he'd earlier proclaimed his hatred for the town and Ryle, it had been out of anger, a childish display that even at the time she'd sensed was mostly for show. Still, staying here had become impossible for her, no matter how well Michael had adjusted. She stood up and smoothed her linen skirt. "The decision isn't yours, Michael," she told him with what she hoped was an appropriate tone of authority. "Think about the good things at home. Things you didn't want to leave. Anyway, you hate this place, or at least that's what you said. I'll be back in a couple of hours. Pack your things. We'll sleep at the shop tonight and get an early start in the morning."

The meeting with Howard took longer than she'd expected. He tried hard to convince her to stay. She wasn't a coward, he told her. Why back out now, just when things were starting to improve? Her business would take off, he was sure it would, and after all the effort she'd put into fixing up the shop... Besides, he added, she'd probably have difficulty unloading that building. Property in Council Grove wasn't exactly hot. The salon had stayed on the market nearly four years before Tracy had taken it. He might be able to work something out with the bank, but he couldn't be sure. She would have to linger in town for a few days in any case. There was plenty of room at the Barclay estate, and she and her brother were more than welcome to stay at his house. He was tactful enough not to ask why she didn't want to remain at the Monahan stables. Or maybe Suzanne had already told him.

As she drove home, Tracy mulled over ways to handle her departure. Should she knock on Leigh's door as if nothing had happened and sing out a friendly goodbye? Should she leave a long letter of explanation and regret propped against the sugar bowl?

The decision was made for her. Leigh was sitting at the kitchen table staring into a coffee cup when Tracy went inside. A matched set of luggage—three pieces, bright yellow and brand-new—stood against the wall.

"Mikey tells me you think you're leaving," she said. "I've got news for you. You're not. I am."

Tracy started for the refrigerator to get a glass of milk, then remembered. Their new relationship didn't allow for such liberties. She sat at the table across from her friend, wishing for the words to come that would set things right. "Why should you go? This is your home."

"Not anymore."

"Oh, Leigh."

"I've wanted to get free of this place, of this town, for most of my life. I'm going to sell Ed my half. I'm positive he'll jump at the chance. With the money I get, I might even go back to school. Learn some new skill, who knows?" At the doubtful look on Tracy's face she added, "You think I can't?"

"It isn't that. These things take time..."

"All the details are in this letter." She tapped her fingers on an envelope that sat, already coffee stained, beside her cup. "You can take care of it all, with Ed. The way I did with you and the shop. I'll let you know where I am when I get there."

"I can't let you do this."

"You'll do it my way, Tracy," Leigh snapped. "You owe me. For now, I'm going to Joplin. I have a cousin there who's going to let me stay with her. You can watch over things here until you find a house. I'm sure Howard Barclay will help you out." She slapped the heel of her hand against her forehead. "What am I saying? You can move in with Ryle."

"I wouldn't. Anyway, it's over between him and me. So if that's the reason you're leaving—"

"On the other hand, why should I squander all that money on an education? I deserve a little fun for a change. I could become a world traveler."

"You could." There was little good in arguing with Leigh when she was like this, numb with her own grief almost to the point of intoxication. The slightest word might bring on the torrent of tears that lay just beneath the surface.

"I'd have to have a whole new wardrobe first. I might as well have the word 'hick' branded on my forehead as show up in the city with anything I own."

Leigh scraped back her chair and stood up, slamming a hand on the table. "Why didn't you just say, 'Leigh, I'm sorry. But Ryle and I have already met and are taking up where we left off years ago'?"

Tracy winced. "I should have. I know that now."

"You think I can't get anybody? Listen, I might not have a face to launch a thousand ships, but I've started off a paddleboat or two in my time."

"I know."

"I'm unattached because I'm choosy."

"I know you are."

"Ed Collins likes me—a lot." Leigh's voice was defiant. "And he's not half bad."

"He isn't half bad," Tracy agreed.

Leigh's smile was weak and fleeting, but it was a smile nonetheless. In an effort to camouflage her red, swollen eyes, she had applied powder and several thick coats of mascara. It gave her the look of a marionette. She started to say something, but tires crunched in the driveway, attracting her attention. A car door slammed and she went to look out the window.

"It's Ed." Her mouth twisted in a wry grin as she turned to Tracy. "What a coincidence." Throwing back her shoulders, she said, "I'm glad he's here. I have a lot to tell him."

"Can't you wait and think about this."

"What do you suppose I was doing all night? Sleeping? You'd better tell Mikey you've changed your mind about flying the coop. He was pretty upset."

"Where is he?" The door to his room was open and it was easy to see he wasn't there. He wasn't in the bathroom, either.

"He's at Doc Tanner's," Ed told them when he came in. "He asked me to drive him there."

"Why?" Tracy asked.

"Search me."

Dreading Ed's reaction to the news that Leigh was planning to leave, Tracy got quickly into her car and sped away. She had enough worries of her own, she thought grimly. Michael. What could he possibly be doing at Ryle's house? He'd been angry with Ryle; he might even have intended revenge. The thought of it didn't exactly inspire peace of mind.

Tracy realized she was driving erratically—from exhaustion, she told herself. And, just maybe, a hint of nervousness. Thank goodness there was hardly anyone else on the road. She finally reached Ryle's place and bumped down the long drive to the house. The pit bull trotted over to meet her, as if it were his job. A black lab mix who'd been sleeping on the porch raised his head and yawned. Stripped to the waist, bronzed back glistening in the sun, Ryle was at the side of the house, setting a new pane of glass in the window. He wiped an arm across his forehead, scowled, and came toward her, holding the putty knife as if it were a cross he was using to ward off a vampire.

"What do you want?"

"Is Michael here?"

"He's weeding the backyard. Why?"

She opened the car door, but he closed it again. "He'll be home when he's finished."

"But—"

"What are you doing? Coming to his rescue?"

"No, I—"

"Let him alone. He has a lot to do and it looks like rain."

"If it rains, he can do it tomorrow, can't he?"

"Nope. We have a contract. If he doesn't finish the yard today, he doesn't go on the trip."

"You don't give rain checks?"

"Not in this case. He waited until the last minute."

"I'd like to see him if you don't mind."

"I do mind."

She paused to collect herself. Ryle would have liked nothing better than to have her screech at him. Then he could play reasonable man to her hysterical woman. "What if it were an emergency?" she asked sweetly.

"Is it?" The eyebrow peaked.

"Not exactly. But I was worried about him. He didn't tell me he was coming here."

He frowned, yanked a handkerchief out of his back pocket and mopped his forehead. "Mike," he shouted. "Time out. Come here a minute."

Until he stood up, Tracy hadn't seen the boy on his hands and knees, digging with a pronged weeder at the tall grasses that grew along the edge of the garden fence. His face was dirty, his hair was shaggy and his back was bare. His discarded shirt dangled from a post, its empty sleeves waving in the breeze. "What's up?"

"Why didn't you tell your sister where you were going?" Ryle asked.

"How could I?" The boy stretched his arms out wide. "She was busy with Mr. Barclay at his house and I didn't have the phone number."

"Good enough." Tracy felt herself coloring when Ryle's all-assuming eyes fastened on hers again. "Maybe next time you'll think to leave a number where you can be reached and there won't be a problem."

How dare he lecture her on what she should and shouldn't do, as if they were idiotic participants in some family counseling TV show! "I didn't expect him to leave the house," she sputtered.

"You told me you'd only be gone two hours," Michael accused. "You were gone a whole lot longer and I had to come here and get this work done."

"It's okay, son," Ryle told him, evidently satisfied as to where the blame should lie. "Next time maybe you can leave Tracy a note. Get back to work."

The boy wrinkled his nose. "It's all done."

"Not the way I see it. Get hopping."

"Yes, sir," Michael groaned, allowing his head to loll to one side as he shuffled back to his post.

"*Yes, sir,* coming from my brother?" Tracy marveled.

"Is there anything else?" Ryle wanted to know.

"Not really."

He brandished his putty knife. "Then do you mind if I get on with more important things?"

LEIGH HAD CHANGED her traveling outfit again by the time Tracy returned. Her gray skirt was now a pair of navy-blue pants and her white shirt was a blue knit blouse. Her hair, loose before, was pulled into her usual ponytail and fastened with a length of blue grosgrain ribbon.

"Did you work everything out with Mikey?" she asked.

"I didn't get a chance to talk to him. He was in the yard working and Ryle was being impossible." She spoke Ryle's name tentatively, wanting to see if she could do it without arousing pain.

Leigh didn't react. She dug through her purse, discarding old supermarket receipts and wads of scrap paper. She uncapped a tube of lipstick and smeared a dab of color across the back of her hand. "I've always detested this shade. But I paid so much for it, I didn't want to throw it out. Now that I'm being adventurous, I might as well go all the way." She let it clunk into the wastebasket.

Walking purposefully to the sink, she tightened the faucets. She straightened the soap in the soap dish and swiped at a streak on the window with a paper towel. "Maybe all this is for the best. Do you realize I've been stuck in this shack my whole life? It's time I left and found out what the rest of the world is like. I've never even been out of the state."

"I know."

Outside, a burst of air, like a miniature tornado, caught up a handful of dust, leaves, and broken sticks and deposited it on the porch. One of the leaves, breaking away from the others, flattened against the screen and remained, as if trying to get in. The coolness touched Tracy's arms, moist from the humid kitchen air, and raised goose bumps.

"Tell your little monster I wanted to see him before I left, but my bus takes off in an hour and ten minutes and the girl at the station said I should get there early. I don't know why. I don't expect there'll be a stampede for seats."

Leigh lifted a corner of curtain and peered out, exposing a threatening rectangle of rapidly darkening sky. "Ryle will probably bring Mikey home if it rains."

Tracy couldn't answer. The ache inside her was growing stronger with each passing second. She couldn't say it now, but she wouldn't be able to remain in Council Grove. With Ryle feeling as he did and with Leigh gone, the town would be gone, too, as far as she was concerned. After the property was settled, she and Michael would leave as planned.

"Why didn't you tell me straight off about you and Ryle?" Leigh blurted out suddenly, tightening her hands into fists. "Why?"

"Because I'm stupid. I wanted so much for you to be happy and I thought . . . Well, you'd fallen for Ryle, so—"

"You *are* stupid. If things were the other way around, do you think I'd have given that fantastic man up for *you*?"

Tracy's mouth went slack. Her vision blurred with her gathering tears. She didn't know what to say.

"I thought about it when you were gone." Leigh's voice sounded soft and distant. "You must care for me an awful lot."

Tracy nodded and pressed her lips together. A strong gust of wind blew the kitchen door against the wall with a slam. Rain began to dot the thirsty porch planks.

"Something really odd happened after you left. I asked Ed about buying me out and . . . he got mad at me. I mean, really mad. He yelled at me. He's never done that before. 'I'm not interested,' he said. 'I've got no use for the place if you aren't here.' You know, it really shocked me."

"It's pretty obvious how he feels about you," Tracy said.

"Well, I knew he liked me, quite a lot, even, but . . ."

"Leigh," Tracy said gently, "he more than likes you. I think—in fact, I know—that you're the most important thing in the world to him."

"Tracy . . ." As Tracy went to brace the door with the back of a kitchen chair, Leigh caught her arm. Tears streaked the heavy coating of powder on her cheeks and her face looked stricken. "I don't want to go. I'd hate all that traveling. I don't want to go back to school and I'd hate Joplin. I adore this place and its leaky faucets and creaky gates. I adore the dust and the kids and the horses. I like knowing everybody and having them know me. And Tracy, I like Ed. I really do. Maybe I even love him. Not the crazy way I thought I loved Ryle—I was acting like a teenager. It's taken me a long time to realize how much I care about Ed. He means more to me than anyone besides my family... and you."

In seconds they were holding each other and weeping. "Don't go," Tracy begged. "Ed needs you. So do I."

"But what about Suzanne?"

"What about her?"

"Need you ask?" Leigh broke away and held out her hands, the fingers stiff, as though they were curved around the girl's neck. "She'll tell Ryle how hard I tried to make him like me—she probably already has—and she'll have him laughing at me."

"Forget about Suzanne," Tracy said with a touch of impatience. "She's leaving town. And anyway, Ryle isn't like that."

"Maybe not. But he'll feel sorry for me and that's even worse."

Tracy shook her head.

Leigh looked at her sharply. "Promise me something," she said. "No, two things."

"If I can."

"Get Ryle back."

Tracy sighed. "It's too late. You should see how he looks at me. Suzanne convinced him that I'm carrying on with Howard Barclay because of his money."

Leigh opened the cabinet and brought out a jar of peanut butter. "So change his mind."

"How?"

"If I had your equipment, I wouldn't have to ask how. Want a peanut butter and honey sandwich?" she asked, plucking a knife out of the utensil drawer.

"No, thanks." Tracy stared at her friend hard, trying to see if her actions and words were still another facade for her misery. "You're—you're sure about this?"

"Positive. Ryle Tanner and Leigh Monahan—it just wasn't meant to be. But Tanner and Whelan. That's another story. It deserves a happy ending. Don't you worry about me, okay?'' Her tremulous smile didn't quite match her brave words. ''Trace, about the other promise . . .''

''What is it?''

''Never, ever—cross your heart and hope to turn into a jellyfish on the spot—tell him about my feelings for him. Promise?''

A picture flashed through Tracy's mind—a picture of Ryle as she had seen him a few hours before, glaring at her, holding the car door closed so that she couldn't get out. ''I promise,'' she said, wondering how she'd ever be able to make him understand why she'd done what she had. But she gave Leigh her word.

CHAPTER FOURTEEN

ONE OF RYLE'S young helpers was sprawled on the porch, eating yogurt from a carton and stroking the mother cat's fur. "I can give you a number where you can reach him if it's an emergency, ma'am," he told Tracy. "Otherwise, doc won't be back till eight, eight-thirty."

"I'll wait."

"It's gonna rain for real any minute. It's just been practicing up." He scratched the tip of his extremely uptilted nose. "Did you come on foot?"

"No. I parked down the road." The Plymouth made too much racket, she had decided. She didn't want Ryle to hear her approach. Surprise was her best—maybe her only—tactic. "I like to walk," she added.

"Yeah?" He looked at her as if she'd claimed to arrive on a spaceship. "Since I got my wheels I don't walk half a block. I hop in the old buggy and zoom." He set the cat down and brushed ineffectually at the white hair left behind on his pants. "Would you do me a favor if you're going to be staying here anyway? The labrador needs his medicine at seven. If you give it to him, I won't have to wait around."

"Just show me where it is and tell me how much I'm supposed to give him."

"You won't forget, will you?" the boy asked later, as he was about to leave.

"No." To ease his mind, she set the kitchen timer on the coffee table, whirled the dial around to ring at seven o'clock and set the pills beside it.

When she was alone, she couldn't help snooping. As she moved through Ryle's rooms, she felt closer to him somehow—being among his things again. Maybe this was the last time, she told herself. Maybe this was closer than she would ever be again.

The house didn't look much changed from her previous visit, the night of the storm. There were still books everywhere, on the couch, on the coffee table, on all the flat surfaces. Some were packed in boxes and others were stacked on the floor, not to mention those crammed in the two floor-to-ceiling bookcases.

The envelope of high school pictures still lay on the low table, as did the photograph her grandfather had given Ryle all those years before. And the pouch with its two small stones. For the third time, Tracy found herself glancing through the dog-eared snapshots. For the third time, she found herself holding the warm stones in her hand. Remembering... and hoping.

She browsed among the books and then methodically examined everything Ryle had put on his walls, getting as close to each object, each picture, as she could. Antique farm implements, crusted with age, hung on one wall beside two colorful Indian blankets. A battered cowboy hat and an old peace pipe shared another wall with a battered guitar. Three framed prints held a place of honor across from the saggy couch, to be viewed by anyone who could make room enough to sit down. Strange, she hadn't really looked at them until now.

The Whittredge sunlit forest and Marc's colorful *Blue Horses* seemed to be the kind Ryle would have chosen. She liked them, too. The Paul Klee depiction of an extraterrestrial type, with a geometric, divided face and unmatched eyes, made her wonder. She studied it from several angles and distances, but nothing helped. Here, their tastes in art differed.

Seven o'clock brought the bell and the end of her self-guided tour. It took her until seven-thirty to lure the lab out from under the bed and until seven forty-five to figure out that the only way she'd be able to get the pills down was to bury them in a good-size chunk of hot dog.

A flash of lightning lit up the sky and she went outside to wait on the porch. Mama cat promptly took a place on her lap and the lab, friendly and forgiving, settled on the ground next to her feet. Never good at waiting, she found it intolerable now as a dozen imaginary conversations took shape in her mind, complete with a dozen explanations for her sudden coldness toward him—and a dozen rejections of those explanations by Ryle. They all ended the same way. With Tracy driving home in tears.

Sitting motionless, staring at the fast-darkening sky, she felt as if she'd been the subject for Ryle's Paul Klee print, her eyes watchful and calculating, one eyebrow cocked, her mouth tight as though tasting something sour.

When the rain came, it came with a vengeance, and she moved her vigil into the house. The TV offered only ghosts, slanting white lines and a spinning picture. She settled instead before one of the bookcases. There were no brightly jacketed new books. Most looked as if they'd been inherited from an ancient relative or gleaned from countless trips to dusty secondhand stores. Many were collections of Indian legends, myths and lore. And there were collections of fairy tales, most of them with wonderful illustrations— marked "with love from Grandmother Tanner." Tracy glanced through an encyclopedia of birds, a volume of Botticelli paintings, then picked out a book of fairy tales and one of Indian verses and songs. She settled herself on the floor, leaned with her back against the couch and began to read.

Nine-thirty came. Ten. Still no Ryle. Her neck ached. Her eyelids felt gritty. Not knowing where to move the things on the couch, she went into the bedroom and lay down, too sleepy to care. She was feeling not unlike Goldilocks—a Goldilocks who had already been through the story several times—awaiting the return of the Three Bears.

The dogs' joyous chorus of yelps—two high-pitched, one bass—awakened her, alerting her to Ryle's homecoming.

The front door opened and closed before she had time to react, and he was there in the house, welcoming his family with apologies for being late.

Tracy remained motionless, waiting for the right moment to announce her presence. It didn't come. He entered the bedroom without bothering to turn on a light. Assuming he was alone, he kicked off his shoes and began to undress.

The shirt came first and fell across a chair with little ado. The pants followed quickly, leaving him to make the trek to the kitchen in his jockey shorts. He hadn't spotted her shoes. Could she possibly slip out of bed, wriggle into them and make it to the door without being seen? Then she could knock and wait admittance. What time was it? Would he believe she'd just arrived?

No chance. After doling out choice tidbits from the fridge to the frolicking dogs, he returned with a glass of milk, set it on the window sill and went into the bathroom for a towel to rub his hair dry. He came out in slow motion and froze in the doorway, as if he had caught sight of her moments before, but her image—out of time and place—hadn't registered.

She sat up. "I didn't mean to fall asleep. I'm sorry."

His laugh was edged with disbelief. "Can I count on these nocturnal visits every time it rains?"

"Ryle, please. It was hard enough for me to come here. I only want to talk."

"You climbed into my bed to talk?" He began to rub his hair with the towel again. "Go talk to Barclay."

"My talk with Howard was strictly business. It concerned the—"

"I couldn't care less what it concerned."

She pressed the back of her neck where an uncomfortable stiffness had begun. "Do you really like Paul Klee's paintings?"

He stared at her. "You came to discuss art?"

"No, of course not." Everything she'd planned to say had flown out of her mind when he'd fastened his eyes, now steel hard and cold, on hers. "I only wanted to tell you that I love you."

"You toss that phrase off mighty easy, don't you?"

"Not at all. I mean it."

"The last time you said it, I believed you and you kicked me through the wall."

"I'm sorry."

"That's another of your stock phrases. All right, let's get this over with. I have an early day tomorrow." He clicked on the overhead light and she threw up a hand to shield her eyes. "Why are you here? A little honesty might be refreshing for a change."

The bright light made her feel rumpled and unattractive. She'd worn mascara that had probably smudged into circles under her eyes and her hair was a nest of tangles. But she plodded on. "I can't explain why I behaved the way I did before, but please believe me. I love you. I did then—and I do now."

"You can't explain what comes over you that makes you turn off." He snapped his fingers.

"I can only promise that it won't happen again."

"I'm supposed to take another chance on your...shall we say, inconsistent notions of love."

"Please listen. There's a reason, but I can't tell you. It...it involves someone else."

"I'll bet it does."

The mother cat who lay curled up on the bed beside her, lifted her chin to be scratched, and mechanically Tracy obliged.

It wasn't the time for subtlety or second thoughts. When he reached for his milk, Tracy lay down again, allowing her hair to fan out on the pillow. "What's the date, Tanner?"

"Why?" He didn't blink.

"I want this date to go on record as being the first time I slept beneath your blankets."

He drained his glass and set it on the window sill again. "More likely it'll go on record as being the night I spanked the living daylights out of you and tossed you out on your tail. You have ten seconds.''

When she didn't move, he growled, tore the sheet aside and yanked her to her feet. Tucking her head under one arm, he raised his hand high in preparation for a mighty swat on her bottom. She tensed, but the blow didn't come.

"I can't hurt you, Tracy," he said, releasing her with an air of tired resignation. "Just go home, would you?"

"I didn't bring my car."

"You didn't bring..." He stalked to the window, jerked open the curtain and peered out. "I wondered how I could have missed seeing it. Got everything worked out, haven't you?"

"I hope so."

In his haste, he stumbled over one of her shoes and struck his shin against the bed frame. Uttering an imaginative curse, he dragged a pair of striped pajamas out of a dresser drawer and hurled them at her.

"May I shower first?" The time it would take her to shower would give him a chance to reconsider. Hearing the water run and seeing her shadow move across the wall—if she left the bathroom door strategically ajar—might arouse some tantalizing visions of what could be.

"If you want a shower, step outside. It's still raining." He threw a pillow at her and followed it with a quilt. "You're not getting my bed. Sleep on the couch."

"How can I? It's full of—I don't know—things."

"There's a rolled-up sleeping bag in the corner, then. Use that."

"Thank you for your gracious hospitality."

"I'd say 'any time,' but you might take me up on it. Now go to bed."

"I do love you, Ryle," Tracy blurted out, not moving. "I have since the night of our cookout. And even before then. But that night, when we were sitting by the fire and you were holding me and pointing out the stars, I knew there was no denying it."

"You loved me then," he said grimly.

"Yes."

"And the day after? In my office."

"Then, too."

"What kind of a fool do you take me for?"

"Ryle, please listen to me. I've just made a very difficult decision. I only hope it's the right one—for a change." Tracy drew in a shuddering breath, and mentally begged Leigh's forgiveness. But there was no choice and surely she could trust her friend to understand that. *No choice.* "Ryle, the reason I backed off from you was . . . Leigh."

"Leigh?" His brow knotted in bewilderment.

"Leigh was in love with you—or thought she was . . ." And then the whole story tumbled out, tentatively at first. From Leigh's announcement that there was a man in her life, to her own surprise in learning who that man was. The words came more easily then, and she explained how she'd battled within herself—torn between her love for him and her concern for Leigh.

But the only effect her story had on him was to make him even angrier. "What gave you the right to design my life for me?" he shouted. "I'm very fond of Leigh and there isn't much I wouldn't do for her. But I don't love her."

"I know."

"Whatever she may have felt for me, I doubt it was love. Gratitude, maybe, for charging to the rescue whenever one of her animals got sick. But that's all it could have been."

"Actually, I think it was more along the lines of infatuation, a teenage crush," Tracy said in a matter-of-fact voice. She was momentarily surprised when he reddened at the suggestion.

"Well, even if that's true," he said quickly, "these things never go very deep or last very long."

"I know."

"Stop saying you know. You were willing to sacrifice *us* because you didn't have the courage to tell your friend the truth. How could you do that to Leigh? How could you do it to me and to yourself?"

He paused, then shook his head. "Tracy, you were wrong. How can you expect me to accept your love as the real thing when you toss it aside so easily? How can you expect me to trust you?" He turned away before she could answer. "Go to bed, Tracy. It's late."

Realizing the hopelessness of saying any more, she got up and walked slowly into the living room. As she nestled into the sleeping bag, she called out, "I read one of your books. It was a book of Indian poetry and songs."

"So?"

"It struck me as odd. There were songs of war, songs of worship and songs about the beauties of nature. But none about love or about the relationship between a man and a woman."

"There's nothing odd about that." His voice was low and resonant and Tracy could hear the springs creak as he shifted in his bed. "The Blackfoot doesn't write many love songs. Love is considered to be a kind of spell. It takes the control of his life out of his hands and puts it into the hands of another person. That scares the hell out of him—as well it should. Go to sleep."

"I read another of the books, too."

He groaned and the springs creaked again.

"There was a fairy tale in it about a prince disguised as a beggar. He fell in love with a princess."

"That's a new twist," he said, his voice heavy with sarcasm.

"To find out whether his love for her was true, she gave him three terribly difficult things to do. He did them all, despite the hardships and dangers, then she believed him."

"The moral is?"

Tracy sat up and looked toward the partly open bedroom door. "Can't we do the same thing in reverse? You give me three things to do, and I'll do them."

He was quiet for a long moment. There was only the sound of the dogs scratching. "Anything?"

"Yes." Hope made her voice small and breathy.

"Okay. One—wake up tomorrow morning early and get dressed without disturbing me. Two—get the devil out of here. And three—don't come back."

She lay down again and pulled the quilt up to her chin, though she wasn't cold. How sad it was, she thought. Just as she had gained a sense of belonging and of being accepted—just as she was beginning to feel that she was part of Council Grove again, the person whose acceptance meant the most was rejecting her. Her life here was over before it had even begun.

A flash of lightning gave her a bright-as-day glimpse of the room again and the sly, off-line eyes in the Klee painting. She turned her back to it.

For what seemed to be hours, she listened to the ticking of the clock, the soft padding of the lab's feet as he made his nightly rounds, the rattling of dry food in the cats' dish as one of the animals satisfied its craving for a late snack. Over all the house sounds came the keening of the wind and the regular crash of thunder.

She wouldn't be able to sleep. Why should she try? At the crack of dawn, she wanted to be on her way as Ryle had requested. Wrapped in the sleeping bag, she sat by the window, as insensate as the white rocks that bordered the flower bed.

"Does the storm bother you?" Ryle's voice sliced through the darkness so close behind her and so unexpectedly that she started, allowing the bag to drop around her. "I didn't hear you."

"Why aren't you asleep?"

She shook her head but didn't say anything.

"Are you afraid?"

Again she shook her head.

"You take the bed," he said, offering her his hand. He wore just the bottom half of a pair of striped pajamas exactly like the ones she had on. Except she wore only the top. They were a pair of bookends in a party shop.

"I'm fine here."

"It makes no sense for you to shiver out here alone. Come on. I'll sit with you for a while."

An hour ago, or two, she would have leaped at the offer. She'd have feigned terror like the witless heroine in the most 'B' of B movies. Now she was beyond that. "I said I wasn't afraid."

"Well, I am."

She looked up at him, not understanding.

His face was half in darkness and half in light and his eyes were as hollow as if he were the subject in an El Greco painting. "I'm afraid that if it ends here tonight because of my bullheadedness I'll regret it for the rest of my life. I love you, Tracy. I always will. We'll work things out, whatever it takes." He held out his hand again, and this time she took it.

In his arms now, her lips grazing the firmness of his chest, she nuzzled against him, as the mother cat nuzzled when she wanted to be stroked. "There's nothing to work out," she whispered. "Everything is perfect now."

"It will be." He held her closer and kissed the top of her head. "I want to take back my original three wishes and make three new ones."

"Can you do that?"

"I'm doing it."

"What are these new wishes?"

"I want you in my arms tonight, loving me and letting me love you. That's number one." He scooped her up and carried her, shoving aside a cardboard carton with one foot as he went. "I want you there tomorrow night," he said, depositing her on the bed, and sliding to a position beside her. "That's number two. And I want you there every night for the rest of my life."

"Number three," she said for him. As his mouth swooped down to hers, she pressed her fingers gently against it. "The first wish and the last are yours."

"And the second?"

"I'll have to give you a rain check."

"A *rain* check?" The eyebrow cocked.

She giggled at her unintended pun. "There's Michael to consider. And Leigh. I can't disappear every night without explanation."

"I'll buy that." He nodded absently and began nibbling at the side of her neck. "We'll have to make it official."

"Afraid so."

"Do you think Mike will go for the idea of our being a family?"

"I think he'll love it."

He smoothed back her hair and pressed his lips to her warm, moist forehead. "If this rain keeps up," he said, not ready yet to let go of his teasing, "maybe—just maybe—I can be sure of you."

"It has nothing to do with the rain."

"But I only see this wonderful loving side of you when the clouds open up."

She dug her knuckles into his arm. "Enough!"

"Maybe—when the rain stops—we should go out and bury the stones. Tonight. While you're in this mood. We'll pretend it's April."

Drawing an unsteady breath, born of frustration, she slid her arms around his neck, pulling him so close their lips almost touched. Almost. But not quite.

"That way," he went on, "you'll be stuck with me. You won't be able to wriggle out again."

"Ryle!" She tangled her fingers through his hair to hold him still. "Do I look as though I'm trying to wriggle out?"

"On the other hand..." As her mouth grazed a burning path to his, he broke off, forgetting what he'd planned to say. His lips took hers and then it didn't matter anymore.

She found herself spinning crazily backward to the wonderful things that had once been between them—and at the same time, forward, to the even more wonderful things that would be.

Maybe it wasn't April. But for Tracy it was still the night of the Spring Moon...a night that would be repeated, again and again.

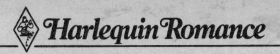
Harlequin Romance

Coming Next Month

2887 LOVE'S PERJURY Mariana Francis
Diana makes a deathbed promise to her sister, Kris, to raise
Kris's baby son. But David Farnham thinks Diana is the mother
of his brother's child . . . a lie she prays he will go on believing.

2888 THE CHAUVINIST Vanessa Grant
Kristy can't believe her ears when, within hours of meeting
Blake Harding again, he calmly informs her she's going to
marry him. But she hasn't forgotten his rejection twelve years
ago, and neither has Blake.

2889 TEMPORARY PARAGON Emma Goldrick
When Beth Murphy set out to avenge her niece's reputation,
she discovers how difficult it is to arrange a wedding.
Particularly when the intended groom is more intent on
marrying Beth.

2900 AUTUMN AT AUBREY'S Miriam MacGregor
Donna's visit to a resort in New Zealand's Lake Taupo region is
anything but a holiday. Especially when the arrogant resort
owner expects her to pretend to be his lover to ward off
his ex-wife!

2901 THE DOUBTFUL MARRIAGE Betty Neels
Matilda is more than surprised at Doctor Rauward van
Kempler's proposal, but but she sensibly agrees to the marriage
of convenience—only to find herself far from sensibly
involved.

2902 ENTRANCE TO EDEN Sue Peters
When Kay's culinary talents are doubted by a handsome
aristocrat who hires her to cater a wedding, she vows to prove
him wrong and be done with him. But he seems intent on
having her around. . . .

Available in January wherever paperback books are sold, or
through Harlequin Reader Service.

In the U.S.
901 Fuhrmann Blvd.
P.O. Box 1397
Buffalo, N.Y. 14240-1397

In Canada
P.O. Box 603
Fort Erie, Ontario
L2A 5X3